# RIDE WIT

M000046018

## DEVILS RIDERS BOOK TWO

## JOANNA BLAKE

Copyright © 2017 by Joanna Blake

All rights reserved.

No part of this book may be reproduced in any form or by any electronic or mechanical means, including information storage and retrieval systems, without written permission from the author, except for the use of brief quotations in a book review.

Created with **Vellum**

*For my Family*

# RIDE WITH THE DEVIL

## DEVILS RIDERS BOOK TWO

I*'m big and mean. I like it dirty. She's off limits and way too innocent. But I'd like to see someone try and stop me.*

JANET

When my career as a dancer is sidelined due to an injury, I have no idea what to do with my life. My best friend Kaylie is dating the head of the Devil's Riders, so I tag along when she hangs out at the club.

*That's when I see him. The one they call the Viking.*

He never says a word, but his eyes burn into me. He watches out for me, even kisses me, but that's it. The man refuses to take the next step.

I know he wants me. I just need to tip the big guy over the edge.

*You know what they say about the big ones, right?*

JACK

I'm big and mean and I don't give a damn about anything but the Riders. But when the fiesty redhead shows up with the Prez's old lady, I'm told to watch her.

*Problem is, I can't stop.*

I want my eyes and the rest of me, on her. She's a pain in the ass but that doesn't change biology. She's mine for the taking, and I'm going to take her up on the offer. For good.

I'm just not sure she can handle what I'm offering her.

**Ride With The Devil is the second book in the Devil's Riders series. It was previously released under a different title. It has been extensively rewritten and expanded. I can't wait for you to read it!**

**Xoxox,**

**Joanna**

P.s. I know I'm not supposed to pick favorites but here goes: Jack is my favorite hero ever. Nick from Slay Me is next, then Jace from A Bad Boy For Summer. And finally Cade from Go Big. Yep, two of them are the strong but silent type and two are over the top, cocky alpahs. So, go ahead and borrow my number one book boyfriend for a few hours! Enjoy! <3

# FOREWORD

This book was previously released under a different title. It has been extensively rewritten and expanded.

I have included the short story Slade as a bonus at the back!

Enjoy!

Xoxox,

Joanna

# PROLOGUE

## JACK

Jack watched as brother after brother disappeared into the back with the sweetbutts. Everyone was so focused on getting ass they didn't pay attention to what really mattered: staying alive.

The club wasn't just about getting wasted and getting tail. It meant something. They were supposed to be a well oiled machine. An army.

But this was just… sloppy.

He shook his head. He didn't have the patience for dealing with women. Not when he had bigger fish to fry.

It had been a while since he laid anyone though. He hadn't had the urge. Some people might say he didn't have any urges, at all.

He knew he could have his pick of the women hanging around the bar tonight. Hell, a couple of them would have done anything to get a couple of minutes with his cock. He had gotten a reputation for being unnaturally large. Not from any locker room talk either.

It was just visible through his pants.

It was kind of hard to hide something the size of a tree trunk.

It was true that he was big, but also a pain in the ass. Could he help it that he was 6'4" with a cock to match? It didn't mean he was offering rides.

In fact, he was way too popular for his liking.

Something about the way he kept to himself only seemed to make the girls more desperate to get his attention. They made it clear they'd do anything to please him. He sneered at a girl with frizzy bleached out hair who brushed past him with a simper.

Maybe it was time to head home.

He stalked over to the bar and put down the heavy mug that Donnie kept just for him.

"Want a refill?"

Jack shook his head. He'd been drinking ginger ale all night, as usual.

"Calling it a night?"

"Yeah."

Donnie smiled at him. Jack didn't smile back. It wasn't that he didn't like Donnie. It was just that Jack never smiled.

Donnie held out his hand and Jack clasped it in a show of brotherhood.

"See you tomorrow, Viking."

Jack nodded and left. He ignored the looks he was getting from the rest of the club and the easy women who were lounging everywhere. He was not in the mood for dealing with them, even just for some head.

He strode out to his bike and climbed on. It was just a quick ride to his shop and the apartment above it. It was late but he wasn't sleepy. He decided to throw the lights on upstairs and work on the roof deck.

Jack was hammering in two by four planks of cedar when he looked up at the sky. It was already getting light out but he could still see the stars. It was beautiful up here.

Or it would be, when he was finished.

He wondered briefly who the hell he was building this for. It's not like he had anyone to share it with other than Dev and Donnie. Hell, he hardly even talked to them, even though he saw them every day.

He would lay down his life for them in a heart beat.

Not that it was saying much. He knew his life wasn't worth much to anyone anyway.

He'd known that since he was five years old.

# CHAPTER ONE

## JANET

Janet stared at her shoes while her father droned on and on about responsibility. She did her best to tune him out completely. It wasn't like she hadn't heard it all before.

Over and over again.

She was mentally running her routine. The last part she'd played in the Seattle Ballet Company. In her mind she marked out all her steps, swooping with the music. It was almost like she was back there, dancing her heart out. Even though it had been well over a year ago.

It almost worked too.

And then her mother took over the lecture, making sure Janet knew how *humiliated* she was to have a daughter 'like her.'

*Ouch. That was a new one.*

Janet tuned her out too. It was better this way. Don't try and make them see reason. That had never gotten her far. Just let them have their say and she could get on with her life.

Whatever that was going to turn out to be.

She bit her tongue to keep from talking back. They just didn't get her. They never had, and she doubted they ever would. They had expectations about the way a proper young lady should sit and talk and behave.

Ideas that seemed straight out of the 1950's if you asked Janet.

Her parents were extremely well off and belonged to every club in town. They had the nicest house in the neighborhood, the nicest cars, and until recently, the nicest little goody two shoes, professional ballet dancer for a daughter.

She almost laughed but she didn't want to get them going again. She *had* been a goody two shoes. Until about a year ago. Then BAM.

Now, not so much.

Janet had never been the sort of person who did well with a bunch of rules. Dancing was different. She was okay with coloring in the lines for the sake of her art.

But other than that, she was always a little bit of a rebel.

She didn't care about what other people thought, not like her parents did. But she didn't want to fight.

Not tonight.

Tonight she was meeting her best friend. She was finally seeing Kaylie for the first time in six months. Since she'd left for college.

*That* had gone really well.

College had not been for her, to put it mildly. She missed dancing too much. After the accident, nothing could quite get through to her. She hadn't enjoyed her classes, the dorms or anything really.

Well, except for one thing…

She rolled her eyes and forced herself to keep still. She was ready to bounce out of her chair with excitement. Not just because she was going to see Kaylie, but because of *where* they were meeting.

They were going *there*.

The SOS clubhouse.

Janet had never been inside the Spawn's headquarters. Few outsiders had. And tonight was her chance.

Her best friend was dating the President of one of the most notorious MC clubs in all of California!

She was bursting with anticipation. She wondered if there would be anyone there she might want to date too. Kaylie had warned her that most of the guys were pretty cavalier about women, but you never know.

Besides, Janet decided that *she* could be cavalier *too*.

She'd been feeling particularly reckless since getting kicked out of college for poor grades. She'd spent a semester and a half on academic probation, struggling since almost the first week of school.

She didn't really blame her parents for being mad about that.

But how could they understand what it was like?

There was no way to explain it to them. College had changed everything for her. Once she wasn't dancing seven hours a day, her curves had blossomed.

After years she was finally a *woman*. She'd always been distracted by boys. Kaylie teased her about it endlessly.

But after all this time, *she* distracted *them* too.

How was she supposed to concentrate on school with so many other things to do? She just wanted to dance and have fun. She'd gotten into the habit of hitting the night clubs almost every damn night.

Of course, she was flunking out!

She peeked up at her parents sour expression. It was painfully obvious that they were still disappointed that her ballet career had been cut short.

It didn't seem fair.

She was the one who'd worked so hard for all those years. And besides, it's not like they had been expecting her to go to med school.

No, they expected her to rub shoulders with the rich art world, get married as quickly as possible and start popping out future rich people of America.

Janet hadn't thought much past her next pair of tights. But she had been hoping, in a vague way, to become a physical therapist someday.

It was the last thing anyone expected from her, but it was true.

She'd fallen in love with the profession after the injury that forced her to hang up her toe shoes for good. Her physical therapist Becky had been amazing and so smart. It was around that point that she'd started to fill in and finally develop- after years and years of waiting- actual boobs.

*God, she loved her boobs.*

She loved the way they looked, the way they felt, and especially the way they seemed to open doors... get her out of speeding tickets... even get her free drinks.

Lots and lots of free drinks.

She tugged her skirt down over the tiny heart tattoo on her outer thigh. It was a good thing they hadn't seen that yet. No reason to send them into the stratosphere.

Especially since that wasn't the last tattoo she planned on getting...

After another twenty minutes of lecturing they finally seemed to lose steam. Janet had heard enough about responsibility and becoming a productive member of society for a lifetime.

She wasn't sure how she was going to fit into this world just yet, but she was sure it wasn't going to be the way her parents were talking about.

Not even close.

# CHAPTER TWO

## JACK

Jack stood watching while Donnie kept everyone in stitches. Donnie was practically sitting on the bar while he told the guys a hilarious story about Dev and Kaylie. He grunted at the punch line, as amused as everyone else.

Jack never spoke and Donnie loved to gab. The SOS's third in command could charm a snake out of it's skin. Jack didn't mind though, he actually liked listening to Donnie talk.

It was a good thing too.

Donnie's story escalated, painting a picture of Devlin as a marked man, doomed for a lifetime of serving his tiny, young old lady.

Making fun of the club President's sudden and utter devotion to a mere slip of a girl was everyone's favorite pastime. The Spawn's all adored Kaylie too so it was never mean spirited. But it was funny, even to Jack.

Especially to Jack. He didn't believe in love, but Devlin might change his mind. The formerly gruff Club President.

It was just too funny to see Devlin mooning over a woman when he'd had the chance to bed nearly every woman in two counties. You would think that would jade a man, make him bored or cynical.

Jack knew better though. As his second in command he knew that Dev had been needing something more than that.

He had for a long time.

After Dev lost his family, the club was all he had. Dev's dad was the former Club President so he wasn't hazed or ever a probationary member. But he was young, alone and just getting his legs on the road.

At 28, Jack was a couple of years older and had taken him under his wing. He'd never told the boy what to do, but he'd shown him by example.

The kid had good instincts from the start. He was strong and smart and fearless, sure. But it was his backbone and sense of fair play that Jack had known would make him into an incredible leader one day.

And he'd been right.

Donnie was mimicking Kaylie accepting a larger than life bouquet of pink roses, pretending to struggle under the weight as he simpered in a high pitched voice. A voice which sounded nothing like Kaylie to Jack. He rolled his eyes.

"And then she squeals 'Oh Dev! For me?'"

Everyone laughed except Jack. He'd been there. Donnie had it wrong.

The bouquet had been at least twice that size.

"Speak of the Devil!"

Devlin eyed them warily as he came into the bar. He took the ribbing the way it was intended, with a wink and a smile. He was smitten though.

If Kaylie wasn't such a good person, Jack might have been worried about him.

Dev was wearing a clean and pressed shirt. That meant only one thing. Kaylie was coming to the clubhouse tonight. That meant everyone had better be on their best behavior, or else.

Jack would make sure of it.

Jack sipped his ginger ale and scoped the bar out for trouble makers. There were always short fuses around to defuse in the

SOS bar room. It was only an urgent matter when Dev's old lady was in the clubhouse though. Usually the Spawn let their guys work things out the old fashioned way.

But not when Kaylie was there. Dev was really strict about what was said and done around her. Some saw it as a sign of weakness, but not Jack.

He knew Dev was a lucky son of a bitch to have found somebody who deserved that level of care and protection. Someone who loved him back. If anything, Jack was jealous. Not that he'd ever expected or even wished for anything like that for himself.

He had been born without love, raised without it, and he expected to die without it too.

Dogs like him didn't deserve love.

He did deserve dignity and brotherhood from the other Spawns. But only through the dint of his unwavering loyalty. Other than that, he considered himself to be worthless.

Well, except in a fight.

Then he came in *real* fucking handy.

Jack stood well over six feet tall and was built like a freight train. With broad shoulders and a massive heavily muscled chest over narrow waist and hips, he was in peak physical condition.

He'd lost the last of his extra padding in the last few years when he'd finally stopped drinking himself into oblivion every night. With his tattoos, muscular physique and streaming long dark hair, he'd earned himself a slew of embarrassing nicknames over the years.

Unfortunately there was one that stuck.

*The Viking.*

He never responded to the joking around with more than a level stare. The joking usually stopped immediately.

He didn't like to be teased, or taken less than seriously. But he put up with it, because he liked being in the thick of it with his fellow Spawn.

His life had been so desolate before he'd been initiated. He'd ridden alone for years, hitting the road when he was just 15 on the back on a stolen bike. He was still isolated in a lot of ways, but at least he wasn't alone.

For the first time in his life, he knew there'd be someone to cry at his funeral.

His brothers.

# CHAPTER THREE

## JANET

*H*ere we go...

Janet exhaled and forced herself to relax as she followed Kaylie into the clubhouse. Years of dance training had given her a rail straight spine. She reminded herself to slouch a little, and to keep her strides short.

Sometimes people thought she was stuck up because of her posture. She wasn't a snot, though she certainly wasn't a shrinking violet. She relaxed her body, letting it sway naturally, sinking into her hips when she walked.

*Do not walk like a freaking ballet dancer!*

She stared around the clubhouse as Kaylie led her to the bar room. The place was bigger than she'd thought. Not that she'd ever seen past the twelve foot chain link fence that surrounded the compound before.

You needed an invite to get in, and the club wasn't in the habit of inviting in high school girls. As far as she knew anyway.

She tried not to look wide eyed, but damn!

It was literally as if the most bad ass, honky tonk bar had been plopped down in the middle of the huge building, far from prying eyes. There was a long dark wood bar with a brass railing, fully stocked, two stripper poles on either end of the room, and chairs and tables everywhere.

And men. Lots and lots of men.

They all turned to look at them when they walked in. Every single guy in the joint gave her the look over. Janet looked around and saw a few *seriously* underdressed women here and there.

She smiled to herself. Her mini skirt and tank top were practically modest. Not as modest as Kaylie's outfit, but close.

Devlin made a beeline for them, kissing Kaylie quickly before holding out his hand in greeting. God, he was cute. Janet couldn't help but be a little envious of the adoring way he was staring at her friend.

There was no doubt in her mind that he loved Kaylie.

Of course, it was kind of hard not to love Kaylie. Janet had adored her since they were little girls playing in the sandbox together. Didn't matter that Janet's family was wealthy or that Kaylie and her single mom lived in a less desirable part of town.

It had been friendship at first sight. Nothing, and no one had been able to keep them apart since.

Well, other than the whole leaving town to pursue a classical dance career part.

She sighed dreamily, wondering if anyone would ever look at her the way Devlin looked at her friend.

The crowds parted as he led them over to the bar. Without a word a few guys got up to vacate stools for them. She and Kaylie hopped onto the stools as a handsome guy with spiky black hair and bright blue eyes came over to take their orders.

"You must be Janet. I've heard a lot about you. I'm Donahue."

Janet blushed a little bit. What had Kaylie said about her to these guys? And why would a tough as nails biker give a shit?

From what she could see, they used up women like tissue paper. But Kaylie was in a protected class, and because of that, Janet was too.

It wasn't just that she was the MC's President's old lady. It's because they cared about Kaylie, Janet realized.

Kaylie was one of them now.

Janet had never belonged to any group. Even as a dancer it had been a mostly solitary occupation.

Her abilities growing up had set her so far above the rest of the local talent that no one had really talked to her. Except her teacher Mrs. Lewis, who adored her. And other dancers in the company had seen her as a threat. Until the accident.

Now she was just plain old Janet Mahoney.

"Thanks. It's… nice to meet you too."

"What can I get you lovely ladies this evening?"

She glanced at Kaylie who smiled conspiratorially and leaned forward.

"Two sea breezes please."

Donnie rolled his eyes at the girly order, making them giggle. There were two other guys behind the bar running around and doing the grunt work but Donnie made their drinks, even adding fresh fruit.

They turned around on their bar stools to include Devlin. He waved to a man across the room and he started over.

Janet's heart did a little flip flop at the sight of him. Now *there* was a biker. Tall and lean and mean looking.

He had long dark hair and was dressed in leather pants and a club jacket, with a black t-shirt underneath. His worn in jeans hugged thighs as thick as tree trunks. And his calves were so big they filled out his jeans. His feet were big too. She shivered as he got closer and she saw his eyes.

No man should have eyes that beautiful. Not in a face made out of granite. And they were dark- so deep and secret that they looked black. His lips were full and sensual even though he looked like he hadn't smiled in a century.

He didn't look to the left or the right as he walked toward them. It was kind of like she was staring at the Terminator, but a really sexy one. She realized she was gripping her drink too hard and relaxed her hand.

"This is Jack, my second in command. Jack, this is Janet."

Her mouth felt dry as the giant turned his attention toward her. She held her breath as she waited for their eyes to meet. His eyes flicked over her as if she were inconsequential.

But then- he paused as their gazes locked.

There was a glimmer of something- *warm* in his eyes. Hot even. She felt it down to her toes.

Other places too.

Forget that he was an outlaw biker- eyelashes like that on a man should be criminal. He jerked his eyes away and that was it, whatever electric current she'd felt leap between them was gone.

He nodded at her, and then at Kaylie. And then he turned around and stalked back to the spot he'd been occupying across the room. He hadn't said even one word.

Janet's mouth must have been open as she stared at him. He was - Jesus - he was a little bit scary! Kaylie giggled and sipped the fresh drink that Donnie had just placed in front of her.

"Don't mind, Jack. He's not as mean as he looks."

*"He isn't?"*

Devlin grinned and grabbed the beer Donnie served him without asking.

"Jack's one of the best people I know. He just doesn't like to brag about it." He grinned. "Or anything, really."

Janet glanced over her shoulder. She could have sworn Jack was scowling at her. But he turned his gaze so sharply that she couldn't be sure.

His name was Jack. And he was beautiful, in an utterly terrifying way. Kind of like a Bond villain. Or a super villain in a cartoon.

And oh, so manly.

She sighed and sipped her drink. She knew what she would be dreaming about that night…

# CHAPTER FOUR

## JACK

He stood by the door, letting his gaze soften as he took in everything at once. One thing kept catching his eye though, no matter how hard he tried to not to stare.

*Her.*

Shiny and bright as a new penny. Not just her hair either. With her long legs and stunning face, she was physically stunning. But it was more than that.

The damn girl sparkled with zest and curiosity. She shouldn't be here. Not even with Kaylie. There was something about Janet. She didn't seem like stuff would just roll off her the way some people did.

She seemed like she would absorb it. Every bit. And this kind of place was the wrong thing for a shiny penny like her to absorb.

She was too good for guys like him to even *look* at her.

"Do me a favor man?"

He nodded. Dev knew he would do anything for him, or the club.

But especially Dev and Donnie.

"My old lady is here tonight, we got to keep things extra chill."

Jack grunted in agreement. He liked Dev's new woman. First woman, really. Dev had never been serious about a female in his life.

You would think it would soften him but instead it made him harder. More ferocious.

Well, other than the flowers and chocolates he brought her. He'd gotten her a leather jacket and a helmet too. Gloves for riding. And a pair of motorcycle boots.

She was his old lady, there was no doubt about that.

"Oh and her friend too. Kaylie said she's a good girl so keep the dogs away."

Jack's eyes darted to the girl. He'd noticed her alright. It was impossible not to. His cock was paying attention, throbbing in his jeans just from looking at her.

It had been a long damn time since he'd gotten hard without meaning to. And if she could do that to him, he knew the room was full of boners.

Keeping guys away from her was going to be next to impossible. Those legs alone could start a riot. Never mind the silky red hair that made his fingers itch to grab it and wrap it around his rough and calloused hands.

He'd use it to tilt her head back so he could ravage her mouth with his.

"She's had a hard time. She's under the club's protection now, too."

Jack raised an eyebrow.

"*Red.*"

Dev laughed and slapped Jack's shoulder.

"I know man, like waving a red flag at a bull. But I know you are up to the challenge."

Jack just crossed his arms and stared straight ahead, going back to seeing everything and nothing at once.

People thought he was stoic, a giant piece of rock. But it wasn't true.

He knew he could bleed. He knew it better than most.

He knew he had to be vigilant. Stay on his guard. Be ready to fight to protect himself and anyone he cared about.

He had learned that early.

# CHAPTER FIVE

## JANET

"**W**hat's he *doing* over there?"

Three drinks later, and Janet could not get the guy out of her mind. He'd been standing alone all night, surveying the room. He had literally not moved in hours.

"He's protecting us."

"What?"

Kaylie leaned in.

"It can get kind of crazy in here. Jack's making sure nothing gets started while we are here."

"Oh."

A funny feeling was settling in the pit of her stomach. He was protecting them. She felt safe suddenly. Safer than she had in a long time.

Maybe ever.

Kaylie was giggling. She didn't drink too often. Janet was feeling a bit giddy herself.

"They call him the Viking. But don't do it! He hates it."

She took another sip, staring at Jack from under her hair.

"Does he ever talk?"

"No. To Devlin sometimes. But I've barely heard more than three words out of him at a time."

"Is something- wrong with him?"

"No. And don't let anyone hear you say that. Devlin told me he owes Jack his life. He's done more for Devlin than anyone. Me too. He's a good guy. You don't have to be scared of him, I promise."

Janet nodded. She was feeling something, alright. But it wasn't fear.

The hairs rose on the back of her neck. She turned and caught him staring at her. No, not staring. His eyes were boring into her. She could feel his eyes as if he were touching her.

Intimately.

The Viking. It suited him.

She swallowed nervously and turned back toward the bar. She glanced over her shoulder and he was still watching her with a faint, superior smile. She doubted anyone could see that smile but her. It was barely there, in the very corner of his eyes and mouth.

Her spine stiffened and she turned her back on him deliberately.

There was something about him that made her nervous. He was so… male. She'd never seen anyone that masculine in her life. He was like a lion or a gorilla at the zoo.

He looked cold and hard, no matter how handsome or chiseled his face was. And that body… Jesus, he *did* look like a Viking! Strong, lean and ruthless.

He made her nervous. Very, very nervous.

Kaylie was chatting about some of the people they'd gone to high school with as Janet struggled vainly to get her emotions in check. The drinks weren't helping.

Yes, she was nervous. But she was also aroused. She crossed her legs and pulled her top up in the front. When she snuck a look behind her, Jack was openly leering at her.

No, not at her. At her legs.

She felt overly warm in the bar suddenly. As if they'd turned up the heat like the sauna at the dance studio where she practiced sometimes. Not that she danced anymore. It was painful to even think about.

She'd lost everything when she injured herself. Her hopes and dreams. But she'd also been freed of the relentless pressure.

Freed from the expectations of her dance company, the press, her parents and herself.

Especially her parents.

She licked her lips and nodded when Donnie offered her another drink. He was lording it up all night, bossing the prospects around. His merry blue eyes made her feel comfortable.

Jack's black gaze did not.

Devlin slid his arm around Kaylie.

"You about ready to go?"

She nodded, a light blush tinting her cheeks. Janet looked away, not wanting to interrupt their intimate moment. Kaylie had said that Devlin was always trying to get her alone.

She'd said that he was insatiable. Janet had begged for details but Kaylie refused to say much. It was obvious that whatever Devlin wanted to do when he got Kaylie alone, was more than a little bit naughty.

It was also clear that her friend didn't mind a bit.

"Come on Janet, I'll drive you home."

She waved goodbye to Donnie as Dev threw a couple of twenties on the bar. He didn't have to pay for drinks in his own place. It was just a courtesy for Donnie and the other bartenders.

Janet couldn't resist one more glance across the room while Kaylie pulled her jacket on and gathered her purse.

Jack was just where he'd been all night. He was staring toward them again. He could have been looking at any of them. Kaylie, Dev, even Donnie behind the bar. But she knew he wasn't.

He was looking at her.

# CHAPTER SIX

## JACK

"Ready to do a run by?"

Jack grunted in agreement. It was late and the scene at the bar was still going. But they were gone, so he could leave.

*She* was gone.

He hadn't stopped thinking about her since she walked out the door.

There were fifty reasons he could not pursue the girl, no matter what his dick was saying. As they pulled out onto the road he reminded himself of them, starting at the top.

1. *She was a good girl. Classy. She would never go for a dirtbag biker.*
2. *He didn't need anyone. He just wanted her for some Godforsaken reason.*
3. *Even though she was friends with Kaylie, who was a sweetheart, he had a feeling Janet was another type of girl altogether. Those flashing eyes screamed high maintenance.*

4. *She wasn't short but she was still tiny compared to him. He might break her.*

5. *She was a rich girl. A normal, on steroids. The kind of person he sneered at.*

6. *She would want things if he fucked her. And since he didn't just want to fuck her once, he would have to give those things to her. And he couldn't.*

7. *She probably wouldn't fuck him anyway.*

8. *But maybe he could try. Make an effort. It would be worth it for just one touch of that silky skin.*

9, *He didn't do sweetbutts, or regular girls. He didn't do women for the most part. Not for a very long time.*

10. *He didn't like messy. Janet was messy. A hot mess, literally.*

He could go on and on. It was a fruitless exercise. Jack knew he might never see her again anyway.

He'd certainly never dare to touch her.

But he could think about it. Indulge the fantasy. He had a feeling he couldn't stop if he wanted to.

They pulled to the outskirts of town and killed their lights. It was a run down part of the suburban sprawl. An area that used to be nice, but wasn't anymore.

A part of town that time had passed over.

They watched the house for an hour, staring at the crappy split level that one Officer Grant called home. He'd been warned that he was on parole with the club. They were probably going to hurt him at some point, but for now, they were just looking for an excuse.

He'd stayed the hell away from Kaylie and the club, not even daring to get takeout from Mae's since everything went down.

The man looked scared, which was what Dev wanted. What they all wanted.

It was better if he suffered, mentally torturing himself.

It was better than killing him, or just messing him up. All three options were still on the table. But for now, the order was to keep tabs.

So they did.

But tonight something new was going on.

Grant had company.

A woman's voice was raised over the sound of classic rock. Not the good stuff though. The soft stuff. Rock ballads that chicks liked.

Jack sneered.

A blond threw open a window, then turned to throw a beer can across the room. Donnie and Jack exchanged a glance.

Fucking Dani.

"Well holy shit."

Jack grunted in agreement.

"Come on, we got to update Dev. He should be home from dropping Kaylie off."

That was funny. It took Dev three hours to 'drop Kaylie off'. He never wanted the girl out of his sight.

Plus Jack knew that Dev was trying to find creative ways and places to screw the living hell out of his woman.

He smirked. Dev had it bad. Jack would never let that happen to him.

He'd never beg for a woman, no matter how irresistible she was.

# CHAPTER SEVEN

## JANET

Janet moaned, rolling over in bed. Her head hurt. Those sea breezes had punched more of a wallop than she'd imagined. She stared at the clock by her bedside table.

The minute hand clicked over to 7 AM.

*What the hell was she doing up at 7 AM???*

*BANG BANG BANG BANG BANG BANG*

Somebody was knocking on her door. No, knocking was too polite a word. They were *pounding*. Like her head.

"Oh God… Come in…"

"Janet, open the door this instance!"

She shut her eyes tightly. She must have thrown the latch last night in her inebriated state. She'd been in another world last night when she got home.

Thinking about *him*.

She'd tossed and turned half the night. Feeling his eyes on her, even hours later. Did he like her? Want her? Or was he judging her and finding her lacking…

She must seem like a silly girl to a hard man like him. Then again, he was loyal to Kaylie and they were the same age. But she was a very different person than her quiet friend.

All she knew was, she cared what he thought of her after meeting him once. Jack. The Viking.

*Argh!*

Who knew men could be so confusing? In college it had been straightforward and obvious if a boy liked you or not. Now she was all hot and bothered by a man who may or may not even know she existed.

*BANG BANG BANG BANG*

"I'm coming! Jesus!"

She rolled to her feet and tentatively walked toward the door. She felt a bit off kilter but found her sea legs quickly. She almost giggled. Being hungover *was* a lot like being on a swaying boat.

She knew because her ballet company had thrown its annual fundraiser on a boat one year. A booze cruise. That of course, the underage dancers were forbidden from partaking in.

She unlocked the door and opened it to see her mother standing in the hallway with a sour expression on her face. As usual.

"Janet, if you are going to live in this house, then I expect you to be up at 7 o'clock."

"Uh… okay mom."

"And I expect you to be a productive member of this household, if not society!"

Janet didn't say anything. She was standing there in her panties and a camisole looking at her mother's face. There was no love there. Just… regret.

Her mother had never wanted children. She'd never said so but Janet had overheard her yelling at her father late one night. Everything that had gone wrong in her life was all his fault.

And Janet's. Just for existing.

"If you aren't going to work, you will be doing chores! I made a list. It's in the kitchen. You can start there."

Her mother turned and abruptly walked away. Janet eyed her bed longingly then sighed and pulled on a pair of jeans and a t-shirt. She just knew her mother was going to make her life a living hell until she got a job.

But who was going to hire her? An ex dancer slash college drop out with zero experience under her belt? It wasn't going to be easy, that was for sure.

She considered asking Kaylie if Mae needed anyone at the diner but was almost afraid to. What if she was a terrible waitress?

What she really needed was to get out of this house. She felt like she was suffocating here after only a few weeks.

It wasn't just leftover teenage angst. She wasn't wanted here. Her parents didn't really care about her. They just cared what the neighbors thought.

By ten o'clock Janet had swept, mopped, and vacuumed the house. By noon she had raked and weeded under the rose bushes. Her mother had hovered over her almost constantly, riding her without mercy.

Janet's resentment had grown to a boiling point around 3 pm, but since her mother had conveniently disappeared around that time, a patch of weeds had gotten the brunt of it.

Now she was just exhausted. She crawled into bed, still in her work clothes.

Her phone buzzed. It was Kaylie.

*Mall tomorrow?*

Janet grinned sleepily and quickly tapped back 'Yes! What time?' She could hang with Kaylie and look for jobs.

> *2 ish? We'll pick you up.*
> *Perfect!*

Janet rolled onto her back. Tomorrow couldn't come soon enough. She knew if she stayed in her bedroom her mother would tell her she was being lazy. So she pulled on her jogging shorts and laced up her sneakers.

As predicted, her mother tried to stop her before she even got close to the front door.

"Where are you going?"

"For a run. You don't want me getting soft, do you?"

She grinned at her mother's face and popped in her headphones, turning the music to full blast. And just like that, she was free.

# CHAPTER EIGHT

## JACK

He held perfectly still as people walked past him, most giving him a wide berth. A little girl stared up at him in awe. He gave her a nod.

Kids were funny. The adults were afraid of him, but kids never were. He would end up with someone in his lap if he sat down long enough at one of the club's family events.

Part of the reason he preferred to stand.

Jack was waiting outside the south entrance of the mall, leaning on his bike. He didn't usually go to places like this. The smell of plastic and perfume made him uncomfortable, as did all the normal people.

The Spawns weren't normal, they were the one percent. Above and apart from the throngs of average people. Separate, and proud of it.

Jack did his best never to mix with the regular folks. He hardly mixed with anyone.

But Dev had asked him to, and Jack always did what Dev said.

Plus, he'd get to see *her* again.

He'd nodded unenthusiastically when Dev asked him if he was free to go to the mall. The freaking mall. But then Dev had mentioned that Kaylie's hot little friend Janet was going.

Hot was the wrong word. The girl was *scorching.*

He'd been thinking about her for two days now. That body, the red hair, those remarkable aqua eyes… those pouty cherry red lips that begged for his mouth and tongue.

The girl was off the charts gorgeous, and that was just her looks. Her spicy personality only added fuel to the fire.

The list of reasons he'd made to forget her had done nothing to cool his lust. If anything, it made him more obsessed.

And hard. Painfully hard.

Jesus, he hadn't had this many boners since he was 15. He didn't like it. It was disconcerting for someone like him who liked to be in control. He scowled and adjusted his package in his jeans. It was already throbbing, just thinking about her.

*Down boy.*

It wouldn't do to walk around the mall with a stiffy. He almost smiled. Actually, that wasn't a bad idea. What would the normals say about *that?*

Devlin's SUV turned into the parking lot and Jack stood up. Then he leaned back on his bike again. He didn't know what to do with himself.

*What the hell was wrong with him?*

Devlin parked and Jack watched as the girls climbed out. First Kaylie, her golden brown hair shining in the sun. A long pale leg stepped out of the backseat, and then another. His gut tightened when he saw what she was wearing.

Janet was wearing shorts today. Tight little denim shorts that hugged her hips and ass. And Jesus, what an ass. Round and curvy and just begging for a man's hands to grip it.

A man could do a lot with something that juicy to hold onto.

She was leaning back into the SUV to grab something- her bag. He swallowed as her sweet little bottom was thrust even more prominently into view.

Fuck, now he was really getting hard. He looked away and forced himself to think about something distasteful. His childhood. Basically any moment from the age of 3-14 would do.

Before he'd been big enough to fight.

It worked. His body calmed down and he exhaled in relief. He raised his eyes again just as they came toward him.

Keep it together Jack.

Don't forget.

*She's not for you.*

# CHAPTER NINE

## JANET

Janet felt her heart leap in her chest at the sight of him. He was here. The Viking. He was looking at her with a slight scowl, as if he'd just tasted something bitter, like biting into a lemon.

Well, there goes her theory that he liked her. Nope. Not even a little.

He certainly didn't look like he'd been thinking about her the way she'd been thinking about him for the past two days. She wished she'd known he was going to be there.

She would have taken more time with her hair, her makeup, her outfit...

Then again, he was looking at her.

As they got closer she could see that he was staring at her legs again. No, higher. He was staring at her, right between her legs. He looked hungry. She almost fell over in shock.

Maybe she hadn't been wrong after all.

"Hey man."

Jack nodded in greeting but he didn't move his eyes from her body. They slid up slowly, inspecting her. She felt her legs getting rubbery as his gaze flicked over her breasts and finally lifted to her face. She licked her lips nervously and his scowl increased.

What was going on with this guy?

Heat pooled in her belly. Just by looking at her he'd turned her to putty. He'd done more to her than any man alive, just with his eyes.

Not that he appeared to care one way or the other. She literally could not figure out if he liked her or hated her. Or maybe it was a little bit of both.

She decided that it would be better to ignore him. Completely. Act like she wasn't melting into a puddle of swooning goo every time he glanced in her direction.

*Just pretend he isn't getting to you. It will salvage your pride and maybe, just maybe it will make him crazy for you.*

Decision made, she tossed her hair and walked into the mall.

"Come on, Kaylie. Don't forget to keep an eye out for any help wanted signs."

She could have sworn the scowl on his face got even deeper when she walked past him. She didn't even glance back to see Kaylie and the guys follow her into the mall.

*Scowl all you want, big boy.*

# CHAPTER TEN

## JACK

This was hell.

He was at the mall, and this was actual hell.

As a Devil's Rider he should feel right at home. But he didn't. He shifted his weight, trying to will his hard on away.

He had perma-boner. Thanks to her.

Jack stood outside the store as Kaylie and Janet tried on clothes. He'd been inside, standing with Dev until Janet had tried on a slinky red dress that molded to her curves. He'd felt like he'd been kicked in the stomach.

She looked ridiculously sexy- like a dancer on one of those stupid TV shows. It was way too provocative. He wanted to rip it off of her. He could picture the torn dress in his hands as she stood naked in front of him.

He wanted it. That crumpled, torn scrap of fabric in his hands. He'd never wanted anything so badly in his life.

Arousal had come crashing through him. He couldn't figure out why. Not only was she obviously a spoiled little headstrong brat, but the rich daddy's girl was going out of her way to ignore him.

Unless… did that mean she liked him?

Girls did stuff like that all the time from what he'd heard. He moaned. The last thing he needed was some little stuck up girl messing with his peace of mind.

Best to ignore her. She'd go away eventually. They always did.

Unless one of the other guys claimed her for themselves.

He frowned, not liking that idea. He did not like it at all. In fact, he hated it.

But that's what would happen if she kept hanging around the club. He was sure of it. He'd already heard some of the other Spawns talking about "that hot little redhead piece." Being a friend of Dev's old lady made her off limits for the rough stuff, but plenty of guys would be happy to call her their woman.

Claim her. Make her an old lady, for good.

Not Jack of course. He didn't want anything permanent. Especially not with her.

But the thought of her with another man irked him for some reason. Maybe he could discourage her from coming around. That would solve the problem. If he didn't have to see it, he didn't have to deal with it.

Out of sight, out of mind.

They came out of the store, Kaylie swinging a bag in her hand. Janet's hands were empty. That meant she hadn't bought that skimpy piece of fabric they were calling a dress.

Good.

He didn't think he could handle seeing her walk around in it. She'd liked it though. Why hadn't the girl bought herself a dress?

That's what girls did, wasn't it? Especially spoiled little rich girls like her. Daddy's girls who were too good for the likes of him.

He followed them to the next store, deep in thought.

# CHAPTER ELEVEN

## JANET

Janet had been scanning the mall for help wanted signs since she walked in. It was a shame her parents had cut her off when she dropped out of school. That red dress had been really cute on her.

She grinned to herself. Jack had certainly thought so.

The big man thought he was being subtle but she'd caught him staring at her almost constantly. His eyes had nearly bugged out of his head when he saw her in the tight little number.

Maybe he did like her, but he had a stomach ache? That's probably what it was. She smiled deviously as she imagined handing him a bottle of antacid and a tablespoon.

"Look Jan- there's a help wanted sign!" Kaylie was pointing to one of the restaurants in the food court. Janet almost rolled her eyes.

*Great. Mommy and daddy would just loveee that.*

It was one of those restaurants where the girls had to wear skimpy outfits while they waited tables. She was definitely not into doing *that*.

That's until she caught the look on Jack's face. He disapproved clearly. He probably thought a girl like her wasn't good enough to be friends with Kaylie. She squared her shoulders and smiled at her friend.

"Perfect."

Jack's scowl seemed to get even deeper if that was possible. She smiled and strode across the food court.

Time to call his bluff, and maybe get a job in the meantime. A job that would make her parents see red.

But anything was preferable to staying under their thumbs.

# CHAPTER TWELVE

## JACK

He'd thought he was in hell already. He'd been wrong.

Jack stared as Janet filled out the application. She was going to get hired, that much was obvious. The manager was practically drooling on her.

Maybe she liked that. She should be used to it by now.

Jack narrowed his eyes. If that's what she was into, so be it. She could wait forever. Jack wasn't going to fawn all over the girl.

She looked overjoyed to be put on display like a piece of meat. The girls that worked there were half-naked. He didn't think a girl like her should be working at a place like that.

She was too good for it.

Clearly though, the manager was thrilled with her. He kept touching her arm and smiling at her. But he wasn't smiling at her, he was smiling at her boobs.

Jack wanted to kill him.

"If you would just try this on in the back, I can take a picture and send it to headquarters."

Janet giggled and disappeared into the back with the uniform. Dev and Kaylie were sitting at the bar with their heads together. They were always like that, totally in tune. Too bad that right now it meant they were missing what was going down.

Jack walked over and tapped Dev on the shoulder.

"Are you sure this is a good idea?"

Dev and Kaylie both snapped their heads up and stared at him.

"What man? You mean Janet?"

"Yes. She shouldn't be working in a place like this."

Devlin looked baffled.

"Why not? The girl needs a job. Her parents are being real hard on her since she dropped out."

Kaylie lifted her shoulders in a graceful shrug.

"They don't need anyone at Mae's right now unfortunately. It's the mall or baby sitting."

Jack didn't say anything. He just walked away to stand near the door that Janet had disappeared into.

He had an unsettled feeling in his gut. It took him a minute to figure out what it was.

He was angry at Dev for the first time in his life.

They were missing the point. This was not the place for a girl like her. She'd be on display constantly and someone would put his meat paws on her eventually.

It was only a matter of time.

Janet chose that moment to walk out of the storage room in the tightest orange shorts and the smallest top Jack had ever seen. It was cropped to show her flat midriff and way too small. He stared at her, his breath coming hard and fast.

The tank hugged her gorgeous tits, pushing them up and out until they practically spilled over the top. He felt the blood rushing to his groin as hot lust sliced through him.

And anger.

The whole place was hooting and hollering like animals at the sight of her. Janet smiled and cocked her shoulder at the crowd, preening. Didn't she realize the danger she was in?

The crowd was like a pack of damn wolves.

And she was the lamb.

The girl was too damn gorgeous for her own good.

Jack had to stop himself from throwing his jacket over her. He was frozen in place, his eyes glued to her, feeling utterly enraged. A group of college guys at a nearby table started chanting.

*"FRESH MEAT! FRESH MEAT! FRESH MEAT!"*

Jack felt his blood begin to boil. Devlin was beside him in an instant. Kaylie looked freaked out too.

But Jack only had eyes for her.

Red. He saw red.

"I see what you mean, man. Come on Janet, let's get out of here."

Kaylie scooped up Janet's clothes from the storage room and grabbed Janet's arm. She had the good sense to look a little concerned when one of the guys stepped in front of her.

Before Jack could move the little turd reached out to grab her breast. Jack shoved him backwards with one hand and then elbowed his buddy in the chin when he tried to intervene.

Without turning Jack drove his heel down into the little shit's foot and heard a snap. The guy let out a blood curdling wail. Jack ignored him and threw 20 bucks on the counter top.

"For the uniform."

It was over in less than a minute.

# CHAPTER THIRTEEN

## JANET

Janet was shaking as they practically ran out of the mall toward the parking lot. Once they were outside she wrapped her arms around her bare midriff. She had worn far less as a ballet dancer, but she had never felt more naked in her life.

She hadn't been expecting *that*. They'd made her feel like a stripper. Worse, they'd made her feel like she was for sale. Like she didn't deserve respect.

*Thank God she hadn't been alone…*

Kaylie helped her pull her shirt over the trashy tank top. She was trying not to cry. It didn't work.

She was fruitlessly wiping away the tears when she caught Jack staring at her. She narrowed her eyes at him, not in the mood for his disapproval. She already felt foolish, she didn't need him to rub it in.

"What?"

"Why do you do that?"

"I don't know what you are talking about."

*"Yes. You do."*

She looked away, suddenly feeling more exposed than she had in the restaurant. The funny thing was, she did know. He wanted to know why she craved the attention. She licked her lips, unsure how to answer.

"You okay, 'Nettie?"

Kaylie was back, putting her arm around Janet's shoulders. She nodded and stood up straight. No harm done. She'd been through worse. Her whole life people had poked and prodded her, both as a dancer and at home.

Nothing she ever did was good enough.

*Shake it off girl.*

She would just have to find a job somewhere else.

"I'm good, thanks."

Devlin looked relieved that she wasn't going to cry anymore. She almost smiled at the way he was already treating her like an older brother. It was adorable.

And it was really nice to know he had her back.

"We better go. I need to get these two little missies home to their mamas."

Kaylie giggled at Devlin as he pulled her into his arms for a kiss.

Janet opened her mouth and said something that surprised even her.

"Jack is taking me."

Kaylie's mouth dropped open for a full minute before slowly widening into a huge grin. Devlin looked thrilled.

She slid her eyes sideways, peeking at the huge man standing beside her. Jack hadn't said a word but Dev and Kaylie's big smiles had clearly irritated him. Devlin slapped him on the back. Hard.

"Alright, man! Have a good night."

And then they were gone, leaving Janet standing all alone with Jack in the mall parking lot. The big man had barely said a word to her, other than to ask her why she was such an idiot.

Typically, that made her like him even more.

He shifted his eyes toward her and raised an eyebrow. She lifted her chin. She wasn't going to let him intimidate her.

"So? Are we just going to stand here all night?"

He grunted and grabbed her arm, pulling her toward his bike.

# CHAPTER FOURTEEN

## JACK

Jack stared straight ahead, trying to focus on the road. He'd never ridden with anyone on the back of his bike before. He could feel her slender arms wrapped around his waist with surprising strength. She had a good grip for such a tiny thing.

That's right. Kaylie had said she'd been a dancer. It made sense with the graceful way she moved with him on the bike, unconsciously leaning into the turns with him.

He'd given her his helmet and thrust her onto the seat, trying not to stare at her spread thighs beneath him. Those orange shorts clung to her body in a way that should have been illegal.

He'd climbed on and started the bike without hesitation. He made sure she understood that he was annoyed with her. That this ride was a one time thing.

All without saying a word.

The mall was a half an hour from town, which gave him plenty of time to enjoy her body pressed against his back. And he was enjoying it. A lot.

He groaned inwardly. It was his *front* he'd like her pressed against. He wanted her. Badly. He might as well stop lying to himself about it. The little minx was getting to him whether he liked it or not.

And for some reason, she seemed to like him too.

He wanted to fuck her. She liked the attention. That was all it was.

But maybe, it was enough.

Maybe he should bed her.

He'd make it clear that it was just the once- one long night for him to get out all his frustrations. Or maybe a couple of times, until he got her out of his system.

That would give him time to explore her, to take her all the different ways he wanted to… yes, that was a much better plan.

He'd taste her first. Then once she was writhing in ecstasy, he'd slide into her body and wrap those long, elegant legs around his hips. Then he'd ride her, as hard as he wanted to.

He'd show her that he wasn't the sort of man to be trifled with. He would be rough, but not too rough. Afterwards he'd tell her to wait quietly until he wanted her again. It probably wouldn't take too long, given the state she'd put him in these last couple of days.

He'd take her from behind the next time. So he could see that sweet little ass up close. He almost lost his focus on the road at the thought.

His mind wandered again. Toward the end of the night he'd be gentle with her. Maybe he'd even let her be on top. She'd look good riding him. Then he'd drop her off at her house and that would be it.

She'd be out of his system. For good.

It was an excellent idea.

*It was a terrible idea.*

He knew Dev wouldn't like it if he treated his old lady's best friend as a disposable lay. Hell, he wouldn't like it either. The girl deserved more than that.

She was proud. He didn't want to humble her. That surprised him. He'd never thought about a woman's feelings before. Or his own.

*Jack didn't allow himself to have feelings at all.*

Best to leave her alone. It'd be safer for everyone. She was too delicate to handle what he wanted to dish out on her. And he didn't want to make those beautiful aqua eyes fill up with tears when he was done with her.

But when he parked in front of her house and stood up, his good intentions fled. She was staring up at him as she struggled to remove her helmet. He reached out and brushed her hands aside, easily opening the latch. Her hands stilled underneath his at the look on his face.

He could tell she was feeling it too- whatever this crazy feeling was.

Before he knew it, he'd hauled her up off the bike and into his arms. He grunted as her sweet little body pressed against the hard wall of his chest. Her breasts pressed into him as her eyes opened wide. His mouth was on hers before either one of them knew what was happening.

*Dear God.*

White hot lust pierced him as he plundered her sweet, willing mouth with his tongue. His hands were all over her, caressing, touching, feeling, until they settled on her bottom. Then everything changed.

He yanked her against his erection with tremendous force. His cock was practically burning a hole in his jeans. It was so eager to get to her it felt like it would chew its way out.

She made a startled little sound beneath him and reality came crashing back in. He tore his mouth away from hers with a soft curse and climbed back onto his bike. He felt her hand on his shoulder but shook it off.

"Wait- your helmet."

"Keep it."

He didn't turn to look at her. He realized suddenly that he was afraid to. Afraid of what he might do.

"Jack- why are you angry at me? I- I like you."

Her soft admission sent an odd feeling to the pit of his stomach. Something twisted open inside him. He pushed it down as hard as he could.

"You don't want to mess with a guy like me."

"What if I do?"

*"Trust me. You don't."*

He drove away without a backward glance. He wouldn't see her again. It was too risky.

If Dev asked him to escort her somewhere again, he'd explain that he didn't like the girl. That she got on his nerves with her flashy ways and girlish laughter. It was a lie but it didn't matter.

It was better that way. Safer.

He drove away, satisfied that the matter was behind him.

But he couldn't forget the one thing that had gotten past his defenses.

She'd been kissing him back like she wanted him as badly as he wanted her.

# CHAPTER FIFTEEN

## JANET

He *knew where she lived.*

That was the first thought Janet had as she watched him ride away. He'd known without asking. He'd just driven her home, as if it were perfectly normal.

And then he'd kissed her. Not a normal kiss. A ferocious, soul deep, toe curling, hotter than actual Hades kiss.

But what did it mean?

Janet had a sinking feeling that she was in terrible trouble. Not just her life, which was a damn mess. But now she had a strong certainty that she wasn't going to forget Jack, his eyes, or his kiss any time soon.

*If ever.*

He wanted her as much as she wanted him.

She knew that now. He'd given her no doubt.

She could feel it in the way he held her, touched her, kissed her with an urgency that had taken her breath away. And yet he was the one who'd pulled back when they both knew she wouldn't have stopped him from going further.

She would have climbed on that bike and followed him straight to hell if he'd asked her.

Maybe it was a good thing he hadn't. Maybe he was trying to protect her from him, the lifestyle, everything. He'd been noble, trying to warn her away.

Well, Janet wasn't having it.

Who was going to protect her from herself and her foolish wish to be near him?

She stared down at the helmet in her hands. She'd loved riding with him. His confidence on the road had been incredibly attractive. Everything about him was appealing to her.

Not just his strong masculine body or soulful eyes. Not just the way he smelled like leather and smoke. Not just his long hair or bad boy tattoos. Him.

*All of him.*

She walked into the house and straight into her room. She kicked off her shoes and crawled into the bed, still cradling the helmet.

She was in trouble. Deep, deep trouble.

But what was she going to do about it?

# CHAPTER SIXTEEN

## JACK

The wrench slipped in his hand. He cursed, staring at the bike he'd been working on. It was a passion project, not for a client.

Something he'd bought years ago, not knowing why.

There was something about the vintage ride- the lines of it. The grace in the heavy metal.

It was a smaller bike. Something that a lady might ride. Not that he had a lady, or wanted one.

But after years of collecting dust, he'd decided to pull it out.

He needed something to do with his hands. He couldn't sleep. And he couldn't have her either.

So he put his head down and worked.

That was his way.

Nothing like hard work to clear a man's mind. Or sex. But that was not on the menu.

Not with the one he wanted anyway.

He groaned, pressing down on his hard on. The one he'd had for hours. Days really. But especially since that kiss. He knew he should just deal with it, but he didn't want to even acknowledge it. He couldn't admit to himself what had happened.

What had *almost* happened. Because he'd been inches away from tearing her clothes off and fucking her on the back of his bike.

Neighbors be dammed.

That was stupid. And Jack was never stupid. Except, apparently, when it came to one hot little pain in the ass redhead.

*Why the hell had he kissed her?*

*And how could she have felt so good in his arms?*

Nothing had ever felt that good. Or felt that right. Not one thing in his Godforsaken life.

It was as if all the pieces fell into place at once. Just from touching her. Holding her.

Just from giving in.

But giving in was the last thing he was ever going to do.

He grabbed the wrench and started working.

# CHAPTER SEVENTEEN

## JANET

Janet leaned back on the blanket and thumbed through the brochure. In the back there were a few pages that had blank spaces for her to fill out. If she had the courage to.

It was all right there, in the palm of her hand. So why was she so scared to start?

*Application for Physical Therapist Program*

She sighed. It was a two year program at the local branch of the State School. The same one Kaylie attended. It was perfect.

And it also... wasn't.

The state university wasn't cheap and she wouldn't qualify for student aid. Not with her mediocre grades and her parents wealth. Plus she'd only done one and a half semesters.

Hardship case? Not likely. They didn't give scholarships for ex-ballet dancers who hated homework.

She was screwed.

She highly doubted her parents were going to help her at this point. She wasn't sure she would take the money if they offered it. Her mother had already hinted many times that they planned to cut her off, well before she'd dropped out of school.

They'd never been particularly affectionate, but they had been proud of her dancing career. Before the accident. Now they didn't seem to know what to do with her.

Or even care.

Janet rolled over onto her back and stared at the fluffy white clouds overhead. She smoothed down her floral sundress to cover her knees. She wondered what Jack would say. Or rather, not say. She touched her lips softly, remembering the kiss from the night before.

She sighed and closed her eyes.

Day dreaming about Jack definitely wasn't going to help.

She'd just have to get a job and go to school part time. Maybe she and Kaylie could get an apartment together. She needed to get out of the house, that much was for sure.

And maybe Jack would be in the picture too. The big, scary biker was softer than he looked. He had a kind heart. She knew that instinctively.

She also knew he wanted her, but he didn't *want* to want her.

"What am I going to do Kaylie?"

Her friend sat beside her, taking notes for her history exam. She put her book down and sipped some lemonade.

"You'll figure something out, Nettie. I'll help you."

"Yeah… but what?"

"You'll get a job and apply to the program and then we'll see. I believe in miracles you know."

Janet rolled her eyes and turned onto her side.

"Right. Just like that."

She snapped her fingers. Kaylie giggled and squirted lemonade at her through her straw.

"Hey! And I was going to ask you to move in with me!"

Kaylie sobered quickly and looked away. Janet's eyes widened. Something was up with Kaylie, that was for sure.

"What is it? You don't want to be my roommate?"

"No. It's not that. It's just that- well, Dev asked me to move in with him."

Janet squealed and threw her arms around Kaylie.

"Oh my God! That's amazing!"

"I don't know. It's kind of a big step. And then my mother would be alone."

"Maybe I can move in with her instead."

Janet flopped back onto her back and stared up at the sky. Kaylie laughed.

"Sometimes I think I'm too young to get serious with Dev but other times… I love him so much, you know?"

"I can tell. He loves you too. You are both really lucky. I wonder if I will ever be loved like that."

"Come on Nettie, don't tell me you didn't find someone at school. You're gorgeous!"

"Ugh, stop. You are the beauty queen."

"I'm serious Janet. I mean you always were pretty, but now, you look like a movie star!"

Janet rolled her eyes.

"Jack doesn't think so."

Kaylie lit up and clapped her hands together.

"Oooooh…. I knew something was going on!"

"Unfortunately, that is not the case."

"Do you like him? I could have sworn I saw some sparks flying."

"I thought I did. But he has no interest in me whatsoever."

Kaylie chewed her lip.

"Well, I've never seen him with any of-the girls who hang around. Dev said he doesn't mess around with the easy pickings."

"Really?" Janet sat up and then slumped down just as quickly. "He doesn't like me though. I thought he did but… I was wrong."

"I wouldn't be too sure. Jack's the most loyal person I know. He hides his feelings though. Still waters run deep."

Janet just snorted. That was one way to put it. Kaylie nudged her in the shoulder.

"What happened? Tell me!"

Janet sighed. She might as well tell Kaylie. At least then she might feel like it really happened, instead of feeling like some sort of dream.

"He kissed me. It was- Kaylie, it was amazing."

"So Jack is a good kisser?"

"Understatement."

"Ooohhhh! And then?"

"And then he told me to forget it ever happened. To forget him. Some bullshit about him not being good enough for me."

Kaylie started laughing uncontrollably. Janet stared at her, annoyed.

"I'm pouring my heart out and you think that's funny?"

"I'm sorry- it's just- oh my gosh - the fact that he said *anything* to you is kind of amazing. He never talks. Especially not to girls!"

"Well, he didn't say much. Just told me to stay away from him."

"That's interesting. Because it doesn't look like he's staying away from you."

*"What?"*

Janet sat up hastily at the sound of bikes out front. She pulled the straps of her sundress back into place and fluffed her hair.

Kaylie hadn't been kidding. Devlin and Jack had just parked their bikes out front and were walking around the side of the house toward them. It was strange seeing him in Mrs. Thomas' backyard with all her begonias in bloom.

Jack was so... big. So intimidating as he walked towards her. His eyes were hooded, but she knew he had seen her.

She closed her eyes, willing her heart to slow down. Then she laid back down on her stomach and stared blindly at the application. She picked up a pen and started filling out the paperwork.

Well, she filled her name in anyway.

"Hey babe."

"Dev!"

Kaylie was on her feet and leaping into Devlin's arms in an instant. The squeals of happiness behind her made Janet cringe. She pretended to be engrossed in what she was doing.

A pair of enormous boots came into view, less than a foot away. Jack was standing beside her, looming over her. He wasn't ignoring her, that was for sure.

That put all sorts of illicit thoughts into her head.

"What are you doing?"

She rolled over to her side so she could see him. He scowled, so she scowled. Two could play at that game. If anything, the gruff biker just frowned even more.

"It's an application."

"For what?"

"School. What do you care?"

He just grunted and walked over to a lawn chair nearby. He sat down and stared at her moodily. She sighed audibly and turned back to her papers. She lifted her calves and crossed her ankles, stealing a peek to see if Jack was still staring.

He was.

Behind her she knew that Kaylie and Devlin were watching the exchange. She could tell from Kaylie's muffled giggles that they were finding the whole situation vastly entertaining.

"Nettie, there's a party tonight at the clubhouse. Devlin said we can go!"

She rolled to a cross legged position and smiled at Dev. *He* was nice to her at least.

"I thought you didn't go to the parties, Kay."

"This is a cookout so it starts early. Things start getting a little crazy after ten or eleven."

Janet chewed her lip thoughtfully.

"I doubt my folks will let me out. It was hard enough to get them to let me out of the house in broad daylight."

She sneaked a glance at Jack who was still watching her. Frowning as usual.

"But I'll ask."

Kaylie sat back down on the blanket with her and threw her arms around her.

"Come on, it'll be fun! Dev says they make the best homemade barbecue sauce."

"I guess, if I am *wanted* there." She slanted a meaningful look at Jack. "I'll definitely try."

Kaylie's mom came out with more lemonade and a couple of beers for the guys. She seemed to like Jack almost as much as Devlin.

Janet ignored them all and tried to finish filling out her application. After twenty minutes she'd only gotten through one page. She was about to give up and leave when she glanced up and saw that Jack was staring at her again.

Maybe he had been the entire time.

He looked… Jesus!

Damn if he didn't look like she'd hurt his feelings! That was a laugh. He was the one who had told her to stay away from him!

He caught her looking at him and abruptly stood up. The next thing she heard was the sound of his bike tearing out.

He'd left without a word to anyone.

# CHAPTER EIGHTEEN

## JACK

**W**here was Red?

Jack was staring at the door of the clubhouse bar. He was watching to make sure Janet didn't show up and ruin his night. He was really hoping her parents had told her to stay home tonight.

She'd stay away and he could avoid her, like he'd said he would. Better for everyone. Just stay away from the girl. It would be so much easier for everyone. He didn't want any complications in his life and he didn't want her.

*God, he was such a liar.*

He'd been in a tailspin all day. First he'd walked into Kaylie's yard to see Janet looking like a barefoot princess. With no makeup, and her flaming red hair loose around her shoulders, she'd looked like something out of a fairy tail.

Sweet and natural and so beautiful it almost hurt to look at her.

So pure that it made him itch to take that innocence, take it and make her a woman. Because she might be nineteen, but she was definitely not a woman yet.

Jesus, who knew a sundress could be so arousing. He'd finally decided he was going to have to do something about this insane attraction he was having to the girl. She'd chosen that moment to be a complete brat and ignore him!

He had been ready to tell her not to stay away. They could have a thing for a little while. At least until he stopped seeing her damn face every time he closed his eyes!

Now she was the one playing hard to get, dammit.

He sipped his ginger ale and stared down at it disgustedly. What he needed was a real drink. It was getting late and Dev had already left with Kaylie. He had no other duties tonight.

The girl wasn't coming. She'd said her parents had her on lockdown. There was no reason he shouldn't indulge.

Maybe it would numb the raging lust and frustration rolling around in his chest.

Nobody needed him for anything. It had been a long time since he indulged in more than an occasional beer but he wanted to numb himself to these unwelcome feelings the girl was bringing out in him.

*To hell with it.*

Jack strode across the bar and put his empty glass down in front of Donnie, who was lazing around back there while the prospects did all work as usual.

"Tequila."

Donnie quirked his eyebrow at Jack but didn't hesitate to pour him a shot. He held up a cold beer chaser and Jack nodded. Donnie watched him as he downed the shot and the beer in less than a minute.

"Another?"

Jack nodded again. It was going to be a long night.

# CHAPTER NINETEEN

## JANET

This sucks.

Janet stared at her open window. She'd been stuck in her bedroom all night. Her mother had been especially annoyed that she'd gone to Kaylie's house without asking, not caring that they'd been studying.

She'd sent Janet to her room immediately following dinner. *Without* her phone.

She'd finished her application, she'd read a magazine, she'd even looked in the back of the supermarket circular for jobs. She thought she might have found a few places that might be interesting and made a neatly written list of the names and numbers.

But nothing could keep her mind from wandering to Jack. She wanted to be at the club tonight. To see him and be near him. She didn't care if he didn't like her.

She'd make him like her if it was the last thing she did!

She glanced at her clock. It was almost 11. Her parents would be in bed. Janet chewed her lip, considering her options.

Kaylie might not be at the club anymore. She shrugged and pulled on a mini skirt and halter top, dabbing some lipstick on. She yanked on a pair of old cowboy boots and quietly slid open the window. It wasn't the first time she'd snuck out of her bedroom window, and it wouldn't be the last.

Five minutes after she'd made her decision, she was running through the cool grass across her neighbors lawn to the street. Only fifteen blocks to the club. She'd be there in no time.

And then she'd see Jack.

# CHAPTER TWENTY

## JACK

Eight shots down. Number nine is going to be the charm.

Jack was leaning against the bar considering the wisdom of another shot when he heard it.

"Hey Red!"

His head snapped up and he saw her, looking tentatively around the bar. He cursed under his breath at the sight of her.

Long silky legs, bare shoulders and that face. Never mind the hair. She was temptation personified.

And the guys were not in the habit of denying themselves.

She looked nervous. She should be. A couple of guys were already trying to offer her drinks. She was doing her best to decline them, he could see, but that wouldn't last for long.

Women did not come in here at this hour looking for a drink. Especially not looking like her, like a rabbit to a pack of hungry wolves. She should have known better.

*Damn it.*

He strode across the bar and shouldered aside two Spawns who were leaning over her. Her big aqua eyes widened as he closed his hand around her arm and pulled her with him to his spot at the bar.

He lifted her up and deposited her on a stool and went back to sipping his beer. His tenth. He thought it was anyway.

Hell, he'd lost count.

He slid his eyes sideways and watched as Donnie brought her a sea breeze without her asking. She sipped it daintily and tried to continue ignoring him. It was impressive, considering he was standing right next to her and staring at her.

He turned his body toward her and tilted his head to the side, letting his eyes wander all over her. He wanted to look at her. He was a man, she was a woman. Why should he hide it?

She finally glanced at him and tried to smile. They both knew she was attracting unwanted attention from every corner of the bar. She was hot *and* she was new. Everyone wanted a taste.

"You shouldn't be here."

"I was- looking for Kaylie. I guess she left already?"

He didn't say anything, just looked her over, considering what kind of trouble he was about to get himself into. She crossed her legs nervously, revealing a long smooth thigh.

*Screw it.*

Jack grinned suddenly. She caught the look on his face and blanched. She thought he was laughing at her. But really he'd just decided to stop fighting it. He was going to have her beneath him. Maybe even tonight.

*Those legs were going to feel good wrapped around his waist.*

She crossed her arms over her chest, accidentally pushing them closer together. He stared at the luscious mounds where they pressed against each other, creating a deep cleavage.

*Definitely tonight.*

He tore his eyes away from her chest and looked at her beautiful face again. She looked absolutely mortified. He could see tears welling up in her eyes.

"I think I should- go home-"

He lifted her off the bar stool and set her on the floor, inches from his body. She looked up at him, utterly confused. He couldn't wait to take her home. He'd denied himself too long already. He took her hand and dragged her through the bar room. But not to the front.

He was taking her to the back.

# CHAPTER TWENTY-ONE

## JANET

He held out his hand for her, his eyes willing her to obey him. She was about to toss her head and ignore him, like she always did when someone told her what to do. But there was something urgent in his eyes that made her pause.

She took his hand and felt a shock at the rough calluses. Then he just grabbed her, pulling her towards the back of the club.

Before she knew it she was alone with Jack in the back alley. behind the club.

He leaned her body against the brick wall, manhandling her like a doll. Then he boxed her in, standing incredibly close to her. She could feel waves of heat coming off of him as she stared up at him.

She was ready for him to yell at her. What she wasn't prepared for was the look of desperation in his eyes.

He was always so calm. But he didn't look calm now. He looked angry. And something else… hungry. His eyes flicked to her lips and she felt her heart jump in her chest.

*Oooohh… so that was it.*

He wanted to kiss her. Again.

She swallowed nervously. She had been waiting for him to kiss her again all week. Would he finally do it? Or was he going to tell her to stay away from him again?

He hadn't been pleased to see her walk into the club tonight. Maybe if she apologized, he wouldn't be so angry with her.

"I'm… I'm sorry if I made you mad. I know now I shouldn't have come."

He just looked down at her, doing nothing. His body was so close to hers. She couldn't help it. She wanted it closer.

Suddenly a smile flitted across his face. It somehow made him look more terrifying.

In a serious hot way.

It wasn't a friendly smile. It was menacing, like a wolf smiling at a lamb he was about to devour. He lifted his hand to her face, cupping it gently. She gasped as his thumb brushed her lips.

"No, you shouldn't have come."

Then he was kissing her. There was nothing gentle about it at all. He was kissing her *hard*. She moaned and opened her mouth under the assault, allowing him in. His tongue swooped in and twirled against hers, taking her.

Claiming her.

Sweet Jesus, Jack was a good kisser!

He kissed her endlessly, far past the brief kiss of the other night. He'd left her wanting then. But now he was holding nothing back.

Not with his mouth anyway.

His hands were balled into fists, pressed against the brick wall above her. He was restraining himself somehow. She knew it. She felt it. She arched her back and their chests collided. They both moaned at the contact.

And then everything changed.

She moaned as one hand found her body, and then the other. He didn't hesitate now. One hand grabbed her hip, pulling her against his obvious arousal, the heat of it burning her through their clothes. The other hand slid up from her waist to her chest, kneading her breast firmly before sliding his thumb over her sensitive nipple.

She felt the world tilting as he angled her backwards against the wall. He bent briefly to pull one of her legs up and around his waist, opening her femininity to his pleasure. He grunted and started grinding himself into her groin, fucking her through her panties and his jeans.

*Oh God!*

She was mindless, circling her hips against him, not minding as he pulled her top to the side and lowered his mouth to her bare breast. His lips closed over her nipple and flicked his tongue against it repeatedly. Her hands tangled in his hair as she realized she was getting close.

Jack was going to make her come. Standing up. In an alleyway.

His hand slipped down and pulled at the edges of her panties, seeking entrance. She didn't stop him. She *couldn't* stop him. She whimpered her need as he slid one finger under the elastic, touching her soft lips.

"Hey! Jack's having a taste of that sweet red wine!"

Raucous laughter filled the air as a group of drunk bikers spilled out into the alley way.

Jack cursed under his breath and yanked her against him, shielding her from their sight.

She stood there, frozen as Jack turned his head and raked his gaze across the group. They left in a hurry, clearly afraid of the deadly looks Jack was throwing their way.

"Sorry, man."

Finally they were gone. Jack held her for one moment longer and then let go of her abruptly. He watched impassively as she pulled her clothes back into order. She was breathing heavily, still aroused. Still wanting more.

"Is there somewhere we can go?"

He shook his head, as if just waking up from a stupor.

"No."

He grabbed her arm and propelled her through the club and into the front parking lot with everyone watching. She didn't like the way he was acting. He was treating her like a bag of trash he had to take out.

She found herself fighting back tears. Again.

"Mike!"

A prospect ran up to them. She knew him from high school. He'd been a few years above her and Kaylie.

He had a large red scar on his jaw. That's right. They called him Whiskey Beard.

She felt Jack thrust her away from him toward Mike.

"Drive her home. Make sure she gets inside and make sure she *stays* inside."

Mike nodded and walked over to his car. He'd been behind the bar all night working so she wasn't afraid to get into the car with him.

But she wanted to stay here. With Jack.

"Wait- Jack- what's wrong?" She stood there, feeling like a fool. Her voice sounded weak and insecure to her. But she tried again anyway. "Did I do something wrong?"

He stared at her so coldly that she dropped her hand from where it had grasped his jacket. But she didn't give up. She couldn't.

"When can I see you again?"

*"No repeat customers."*

She felt her stomach drop as she watched him grab a scantily dressed girl standing nearby and throw her over his shoulder. He didn't want Janet after all. He just wanted to get laid.

And not by her.

She turned away and followed Mike meekly to his car, feeling sick.

Once again, she'd ruined everything.

She just didn't know how.

# CHAPTER TWENTY-TWO

## JACK

F*uck.*

Jack thrust the blond girl away from him as soon as he was inside the club. He stalked up to the bar and held out his hand. Without a word Donnie handed him the rest of the bottle of tequila.

He pulled on it deeply, filled with self loathing.

He'd almost taken her in a Goddamn alleyway! Next to the trash. He'd treated her like *trash.*

He closed his eyes, seeing her tear filled eyes as he'd thrust her toward Mike. Why should she care if a piece of garbage like him didn't want her? It didn't make a lick of sense.

But she had cared. She'd cared enough to make her cry.

*He'd made her cry, dammit.*

He had a shit ton of work to do in the morning, a lucrative custom job, but he didn't care. He didn't care about anything in that moment.

"Hey, I heard you hit that sweet piece of tail in the back! Let us know if you are through with her, would you? I'd sure like a taste."

He looked slowly over his shoulder and saw Frankie K. The red haired son of a bitch was waiting for him to high five him.

Jack's mind went blank. He saw everything that happened next through a haze of red. It was like he wasn't even there. In the back of his mind, he wished he wasn't.

Him grabbing Frankie's hand. Him crushing his hand in his fist. Him pummeling the guy into the ground until someone pulled him off of him.

Not someone. A bunch of guys. He'd find out later it had taken five guys to pull him back.

Frankie was screaming as he held his broken hand on the ground. Donnie pulled Jack away.

"You better jam, man."

Jack almost laughed. As if that piece of shit crying on the floor mattered.

As if *anything* mattered anymore.

He picked up the fallen tequila bottle and stalked out of the bar to the back stairs and up onto the roof.

# CHAPTER TWENTY-THREE

## JANET

Janet crawled back into her window, the frame biting painfully into her stomach. She didn't care though. She didn't care about anything.

Jack didn't want her. He was probably in bed with that other girl right now. Touching her... kissing her like he'd touched Janet. He was a badass who could have any girl he wanted.

He'd been horny and she had been there. That was it. End of story.

She was an idiot for reading anything more into it than that.

As soon as her feet hit the ground the light flicked on. Her mother sat on her bed while her father stood by the doorway. They'd been waiting for her.

*Oh no...*

She wasn't even surprised. Nothing could surprise her at this point. Jack had picked up another girl in front of her. As if she meant nothing to him. As if she were replaceable.

Obviously, she was.

She stared numbly at her parents as they started to yell at her.

*She was a disappointment.*

(That didn't surprise her.)

*She was to be harshly punished.*

(Not exactly surprising either.)

*She was going to be locked in her bedroom until further notice.*

That last one she managed to respond to, rolling her eyes.

"What if I have to go to the bathroom, mom?"

Her eyes widened as her mother held out a bucket.

"You're joking."

"No, I am not. This is for your own good. You will not be coming out until we can be sure you won't humiliate us again. We know where you've been going and with whom."

Janet's jaw dropped. She almost forgot about Jack for a moment. Almost.

"Bikers Janet? Really?"

Her mother's cheeks were red with fury.

"You have humiliated me for the last time, young lady."

So that's what she was worried about. Her good name. Give me a break. Janet's world tilted as her father shook his head sadly.

They stood up and walked out of the room, shutting it behind them. She heard a dead bolt slide into place.

"What if I need some water?"

"There's a bottle on your desk."

She turned to see a small bottle of water. How long would that last? How long did they plan to keep her in there???

"What if there's a fire? Or would that solve all your problems?!?"

All she heard was footsteps walking away from her. Leaving her alone. They didn't care if something happened to her.

They didn't care at all.

She glanced at the window and decided to make a run for it. She could crash with

Kaylie. Just start over, on her own. There was no time to pack. She grabbed her book bag and laptop and ran for the window.

Just as she reached it, her father slammed it shut in her face. From the outside.

She pressed her palms against the glass.

"Don't do this dad! Please!"

He ignored her, nailing the window into the frame. Her eyes got wide as she realized what was happening. Really wide.

He was shutting her in there. Permanently.

Janet sank onto the bed and wondered how she'd managed to ruin everything. Her parents hated her. Her career as a dancer was over.

She had nothing now. No school, no freedom, no Jack.

The last one burned the most. She'd felt so alive in his arms. So desired.

It had felt like she was the most cherished woman on Earth when he kissed her.

And she'd wanted him more than she'd ever wanted any man before. Who was she kidding? She'd never kissed *anyone* like Jack, not that she had much experience. She doubted she ever would again.

She pressed her hand to her lips.

She could still feel him touching her... she felt hot and cold all over, just thinking about it. She still wanted him. If he walked into the house right now, she would beg him to take her away.

To do anything he wanted to her.

*Everything* he wanted.

But he didn't want her.

Jack had made sure she understood she was disposable. One of many.

Kaylie had been wrong. He probably had a different girl every night. The thought burned into her, stealing away any hope.

*He didn't want her.*

She curled into a ball as wracking sobs shook her body.

# CHAPTER TWENTY-FOUR

## KAYLIE

Kaylie stood outside Janet's front door and knocked. She hadn't heard from Nettie in three days, since the night of the barbecue.

She'd heard something happened after she'd left. Something between Janet and Jack. Dev had given her the PG version, but supposedly people had seen them together.

That was good. She wanted her friends to be together. In their own ways, they were two of the loneliest people she knew.

And two of the best. Both of them were amazing people, and she loved them. So yeah, them hooking up was a very good thing.

This radio silence was... bad.

She couldn't help it, she was worried. Janet had always been a carefree girl, stubbornly ignoring the problems she faced at home. Lord knows she had enough of those. Kaylie had watched for years as her family wore her down.

Her wealthy parents had put so much pressure on her to succeed as a classical dancer that it had nearly destroyed her. The accident had done more than finally end her ballet career once and for all. It'd made her invisible to her parents.

Since then, Janet had been in a tailspin.

Kaylie sighed and rang the buzzer.

She dreaded this conversation. If Janet was hiding out because of Jack, she didn't know what to tell her. He was a complicated guy. Devlin had told her that Jack had his reasons for being so solitary, but he wouldn't tell her why. Either way, she didn't want her friend to be hurt any more than she was already.

"Yes?"

Janet's dad was at the door. He looked over his shoulder nervously.

"Is Janet at home? I haven't heard from her in a few days."

"That's because she lost phone privileges."

Kaylie frowned and shifted her weight on her legs.

"Can I see her please?"

He shook his head.

"You shouldn't be here, Kaylie."

*"Who's there?"*

A shrill voice came from further inside the house. Janet's mother appeared in the doorway beside her dad. She looked crazed.

"Get out of here you tramp! I know you're the one who took my daughter to that- that place!"

Kaylie stepped backwards in shock. What was wrong with them? Where was her friend?

"Where's Janet? I want to talk to her."

"You can't talk to her."

Kaylie lifted her chin. Mrs. Mahoney was freaking her out but she would not abandon her friend. Their words meant nothing compared to her love for Janet.

"Why not?"

"You are a bad influence, that is why! Stay away from her! And you can tell that giant who keeps driving by to stay away!"

"Giant?"

"The criminal with the long hair and the devil bike!"

They must mean Jack. That was interesting. He'd been driving by Janet's house? Since when?

What the heck had happened between them?

Kaylie wanted to get away from these horrible people as quickly as possible but she had to find out where her friend was. Thankfully Janet's mom disappeared back into the house.

"Please Mr. Mahoney. Where is she?"

He glanced over his shoulder and smiled apologetically.

"She's in her room. But she's not coming out any time soon."

"Her room? You are locking her up like a criminal?"

He looked ashamed for a moment.

"Sorry Kaylie."

He closed the door in her face. Kaylie stood there wondering what the heck was going on. Then she squared her shoulders.

She knew where Janet's room was. No one could stop her from peeking in the window.

She snuck along the side of the house and stared aghast at the hastily nailed shut window frame. They really were treating Janet like a criminal. Kaylie shuddered, sympathy twisting her guts.

She might have lost her dad early on, but he'd loved and protected her. So had her mom.

Growing up she'd thought her well off friend had the best life. The big house, two parents... Kaylie had figured out that it wasn't so simple a long time ago.

Now she realized just *how* wrong she had been all those years.

She knocked tentatively on the window. She tried to see into the room but it was hard without any lights on inside. Janet's face appeared in the window. There were circles under her pretty blue eyes.

She looked awful.

Janet held a finger to her lips signaling silence. Kaylie nodded and waited while Jan disappeared from the window. She was back after a few moments, holding up a piece of paper with hastily scribbled words.

*Three days.*

"You've been in there for three days?"

Janet nodded and wrote something on the back of the page.

*Scared. No food or water.*

Kaylie covered her mouth with her hand, horrified. Janet's head disappeared from sight for a moment. She reappeared in the window with a fresh piece of paper.

*'I need to get out of here.'*

Kaylie nodded and mouthed 'I'll be back later! Let me talk to Dev.'

She wasn't sure if her friend understood her. She ran across the lawn, pulling her cell phone from her pocket. Dev would help her figure out what to do.

They had to help her. They had to save Janet.

# CHAPTER TWENTY-FIVE

## JACK

Misery. Pure misery.

He stared at the beer in his hand. He'd been drinking it like water. Trying to fight the urge to go to her.

Janet had not answered his texts or come out of her house when he slowly drove down her street.

He finished the beer and grabbed another.

He would not ride past her house again. It was stupid. It was something a fucking teenager would do.

Just leave the girl alone.

But he couldn't.

He felt like he was tearing up inside. The look on her face when he'd pushed her away... he'd hurt her.

She'd cared enough that he had hurt her.

At the same time he hurt himself.

He'd thought that she'd be confused and that was all. No good girl in her right mind would want to be with him, for real. She was just sowing her wild oats, and he was trying to keep her from getting hurt.

From getting dirty, just by being near him.

It was the hardest damn thing he'd ever done, and it had backfired. He was still tied up in knots, wanting her more than ever.

And now she hated him. Thought he was only using her. Thought he wanted somebody else more.

What a cruel joke.

Nothing could be further from the truth. She was the only one he wanted. The only one he'd *ever* wanted like this.

It felt like he was being twisted into two halves. The smart Jack who should be glad that she hated him. And the Jack that wanted to tear the world apart, just to get to her.

Didn't matter that she was too good for him.

He wanted her anyway.

And now, it was too late.

He threw his beer against the wall. It smashed, spraying his tools with foamy white beer.

He stared at it, breathing hard.

Then he walked to the fridge in his studio and pulled out another one.

Maybe if he kept drinking, this ache inside him would fade.

Just a little.

Maybe it would be enough.

# CHAPTER TWENTY-SIX

## JANET

This is a very, very bad idea.

Janet closed her eyes and tensed her body, ready to leap out of the way. She was holding her desk chair in the air, barely able to keep it up with her trembling arms. She was already so weak from lack of food but she could do this.

She *had* to do this.

Her parents had left her in there for almost four days now. Four days with out food or water. Janet was starting to think they weren't ever going to let her out.

Tears stung her eyes.

She'd always known her mother didn't really love her, but to do this to her? And her father, weak as he was, he'd cared a little bit. She'd thought he had anyway. Apparently she'd been wrong.

Just like she'd been wrong about Jack.

She'd thought he cared about her. More than just wanting to take her to bed. He'd acted so protective of her when those guys had stepped to her at the mall.

But he'd just been doing what he did. He was like a medieval knight in that way. A hero who always did the right thing. It didn't mean he cared.

Nobody really cared about her.

She swallowed back the sob that caught in her throat. No time for tears. She was on her own now, once and for all. She had to do this herself. She was strong. She's survived shin splints and bloody toes on a weekly basis when she was dancing. She'd survived the loss of her chance to be a prima ballerina... the one thing she loved doing most in the world, the thing that defined her.

She'd taken on of one the Spawn's toe to toe for God's sake.

She could do this.

She knew Kaylie would try to help her but she didn't know how or when. Maybe once she was on her feet. But what could Kaylie really do?

No, Janet was on her own in this. Kaylie couldn't solve this disaster. She was no match for Janet's evil witch of a mother. She said a little prayer of thanks to God for giving her one true friend.

Her only friend in the world.

Then she swung the chair back over her head and threw it at the window.

# CHAPTER TWENTY-SEVEN

## JACK

R*ed...*

He cracked his eyes open and tried to shake off the dream. She'd been there, telling him she wanted him. Begging him to take her in his arms and-

Well, fuck if that wasn't the worst possible time to wake up from a dream.

Jack sat up. He was on the roof with the worst hangover he'd had in his life. No, wait, that was yesterday. Or the day before.

Today was the worst hangover anyone had had, *ever, in* the Goddamn history of man kind. He moaned and rolled over to a seated position. It was the fourth day of his bender.

He picked up the empty tequila bottle and grimaced. He needed a cup of coffee. He needed a *shower*.

He needed a shower with coffee instead of water.

"Jack man, you up there? Come down! We gotta talk to you."

Dev was calling him. He stood unsteadily and headed to the roof hatch. He flung it open and took the service ladder down to the main level.

When he got downstairs, a terrible feeling of foreboding came over him. He rubbed his head, wondering if it was just from the abuse he'd heaped on his liver. But he couldn't shake the feeling.

Something was wrong. Something was very, very wrong.

"We're out back!"

Kaylie and Dev stood in the back alley. She looked distraught. Hell, even Dev looked worried about something.

"Man, you look like shit."

Jack ignored the comment. He just waited. But they looked at each other, neither of them speaking. Finally, he spoke.

"What is it?"

Kaylie stepped forward nervously, as if she weren't sure she should be telling him something. He stood there silently, watching her decide what to say. She swallowed and finally opened her mouth.

"It's Janet."

He said nothing, fully expecting her to tear into him for what had happened in the alley. What had *almost* happened.

He almost laughed. He should have just taken her up against the wall. Then maybe she'd be out of his system by now.

That was a joke. Nothing would do that. He knew that now.

God knows the booze hadn't blotted her from his mind.

She was it for him, and he'd blown it.

"I don't know if there's anything going on with the two of you, or if you care about her but..."

He looked at Dev over her shoulder to see if his friend was mad at him. How was he supposed to explain *this* fiasco to him? To anyone?

He had taken the sweetest, fieriest, most beautiful girl in the world, and made her hate him. And he didn't blame her one bit.

"There isn't."

Kaylie stared at him.

"There isn't anything going on."

"Okay. I just thought maybe you wanted to help her. After what happened at the mall.

Even if there isn't... I know she likes you Jack."

He blinked. They weren't yelling at him.

And she said Janet liked him, She did, did she? He felt a tiny flicker of something foreign.

Hope. It was hope.

So she still liked him. She must be insane. But he didn't care. He'd take her, if she was still willing.

No holding back this time.

"Where is she?"

He stared at Kaylie with one eyebrow raised. Even that movement was painful in his recently inebriated state. Didn't matter.

He wanted to go get Janet. Now. But instead of telling him where to find her, Kaylie let out a deep breath.

"I'm scared for her."

*"What?"*

He was prepared for her to tell him that Janet had gotten herself into trouble. Fine. He'd help her.

He was prepared for her to tell him that Janet was angry at him and wouldn't come to the clubhouse. Even better. He'd beg her forgiveness.

He was not prepared for what Kaylie said next.

Not at all.

"Her parents found out she's been hanging around the clubhouse. They-"

*"They what?"*

"They locked her in her room with no food or water. It's been three days at least- maybe four and- "

*"WHAT?"*

"She hasn't had any food or water in days. I don't even know if they care if she lives or dies at this point. I was going to call the police but Dev said-"

He closed his eyes and felt the deepest rage he'd ever felt in his life. His sweet girl, punished for hanging around *him*.

He roared. There was no other word for the sound that came out of his mouth.

Then he climbed onto his bike, and rode.

# CHAPTER TWENTY-EIGHT

## JANET

"I'm here about the opening?"

The woman looked Janet over, an odd gleam in her eye. The place was clean enough looking, if not the swanky spa she'd been expecting. And it was the last place on her list.

She needed a job, and this was her last hope.

Even if giving massages was not physical therapy, it was related, right?

Janet looked around while the woman fished out some paperwork. She had thought this was a beauty spa, but the only people who had walked out so far were men.

Weird.

"Address?"

"Uh... I'm sort of between permanent addresses."

The woman smiled wider.

"Emergency contact?"

Janet's stomach twisted. If you asked her a few days ago she would have said Kaylie. Or even Jack. But it was time for Janet to stand on her own two feet.

And Jack wasn't even a friend anymore. That ship had sailed.

She was alone and she was just going to have to get used to it.

"I don't have one."

"I see. Let me get you a glass of water while you finish filling this out."

Janet sat in the uncomfortable looking plastic chairs. She shifted in her seat. It was ironic to have uncomfortable chairs in the waiting room for a massage place.

Anyone would need a rub down after waiting in this place.

She took the glass of water from the woman, taking a dainty sip. She picked up the pen and filled in her name and phone number, even though she didn't *have* a phone anymore.

Her parents had made sure of that.

She rubbed her eyes, noticing the strong disinfectant smell all of a sudden. She stared at the paper but all the words were blurry.

She took another sip of water and tried to stand.

"Are you alright miss?"

"I'm-"

She stumbled and sat back down again.

"I don't feel right."

The woman smiled at her coldly.

"I know, dear."

# CHAPTER TWENTY-NINE

## JACK

Jack broke about fifty laws in the fifteen block ride to Janet's house. He was angrier than he'd ever been in his life. And that was saying something.

They'd trapped her. They'd locked up his Jan.

He was going to murder someone if they'd hurt one hair on her head.

He was off his bike and at the front door less than five minutes after Kaylie had told him what was happening. He banged his fist on the front door until a man in his early 50's opened it. He looked terrified when he saw Jack looming in the doorway.

"Where's Janet?"

"She's gone."

A pinched face woman appeared behind him.

"You're one of the biker scum that she's been hanging around with. Get out of here before I call the police!"

A voice inside Jack screamed 'I'M NOT SCUM!' with tremendous force. He'd never heard that voice before. He'd never thought for a minute that he was worth anything.

Until her.

"You can have her. Tell that little hussy that she's no longer welcome here!"

God, he wanted to wring their necks. How could they be so stupid? She was better than all of them.

A thousand times better.

How could they not take care of something so beautiful and precious? How could they do anything but protect her? Cherish her?

She was so special. So daring. So brave.

*And fragile.*

Janet had convinced him she was tough, along with the rest of the world. But it wasn't true. She was strong in her way, that was true. She'd had to be.

But there was a vulnerability about her he'd sensed and chosen to ignore. He'd known she needed a friend. He'd known it deep down. Now that he'd met her parents he had no doubt where that vulnerability came from.

They'd mistreated her. Endangered her. Ignored her cries for help. He felt sick to his stomach imagining her in her room, hungry and thirsty and alone.

No. That was wrong.

*He* was the one who left her alone when every fiber of his being had been telling him to take care of her, nurture her, protect her.

*Love her.*

He did something he rarely did. Something he rarely *had* to do. He made himself look deliberately intimidating, leaning forward to sneer at Mr. Mahoney.

*"Where is she?"*

Janet's mother stepped forward. She looked like his beautiful Janet, but distorted in a fun house mirror. She must have been gorgeous once. Before bitterness twisted her features. No wonder Janet's dad was so whipped.

"She ran away. Maybe if we're lucky she'll never come back."

He pushed her out of the way and stalked into the house.

"Show me her room."

Her father eyed him warily and wisely decided to humor him. He led him down the hallway to a door with a massive deadbolt on the outside. And hooks, just to make sure the door wouldn't open from the inside.

Jack was horrified when he saw the size of that deadbolt. Janet was a girl, not a horse or a criminal. She hadn't stood a chance.

He stepped inside the room and winced. It smelled horrible in here. He saw a bucket full of piss and shit in the corner. He closed his eyes.

They'd left her alone with a bucket.

They'd made her sit in here, with her own offal.

This was his fault. All his fault. He's the one they didn't want her hanging around with.

He should have left her alone to begin with. Or claimed her for good. He should have taken care of her. Not this bullshit waffling he'd been doing. Fighting himself every step of the way.

Now she was the one paying the price.

It wasn't right.

*"Get out."*

Her father was lifting the bucket when Jack snapped the order at him. He hesitated then awkwardly carried the offending container out of the room. Jack blew air out through his nose and looked around the room. He could hear them arguing out there. The woman wanted to call the police but the man was trying to convince her not to.

Everything about the room reminded him of her.

The room looked like a sanctuary. With parents like that, it was no wonder she'd created her own world in here. Posters of far away places covered the walls, all interspersed with stunning photos of dancers. Slender girls with long legs and frilly costumes.

They were supposed to be beautiful and strong.

None of them held a candle to her.

A rose colored scarf covered her lamp, lending the room an ethereal glow. He turned and saw her bed. It was a mess, with blankets and sheets everywhere. As if she'd tossed and turned on it. All alone.

Except for his helmet.

He moaned out loud, realizing she'd been sleeping with it. He closed his eyes again, feeling a sharp sting of regret. He regretted everything he'd done since he met her.

Except kissing her. He could never regret that.

He stared at the window. She'd smashed it open after three and a half days trapped in this airless room with no food or water. Or comfort.

While he'd been drinking himself into oblivion, she'd been in here, alone and afraid. Sharp pieces of glass stuck out in every direction. It was a miracle that she hadn't cut herself.

Maybe she had. Maybe she was bleeding to death in an alley somewhere. If she died, he'd never get to tell her he was sorry.

He'd never get to tell her he cared.

He had to find her. Now. But how?

She could be anywhere. Kaylie was her best friend and even she had no idea where Janet could have gone. It's not like she had anyone else to run to.

Except him. She had him and she didn't even know it.

If he'd played his cards differently, she would have come to him for help... instead she was out there, in God only knows what kind of danger. He spun in a circle, scanning the room for a sign. There was nothing. If she'd taken anything with her it couldn't have been much.

Then he saw it. On the floor next to her desk was a piece of paper. He picked it up.

It was a list of names and numbers. He frowned and then realized they were jobs she meant to apply to. He read it quickly and sucked in his breath. The third item on the list was a body work place. She'd probably thought it was a place to learn physical therapy.

But she was wrong.

Jack knew what it really was.

It was part of an underground prostitution ring run by another club. The Vipers.

They'd love a pretty little thing like Janet. Lost and alone and so beautiful it made your insides ache to look at her.

If they got their hands on her... they'd never let her leave. He crumbled the paper in his fist and left, fear making his heart pound furiously in his chest.

He had to save her.

He had to make this right.

# CHAPTER THIRTY

## JANET

*T*hink Janet. Think. How do you get out of this. You have to get out, before they-

Janet closed her eyes tightly, refusing to even think about what they wanted to do. She was curled into a ball on the floor, trying to protect her body in case they touched her again. She waited ten minutes in that position, making sure they were gone for real.

She had been here for at least twelve hours. Enough time to wake up in lingerie, and be held down while the owner explained 'the rules' to her.

They wanted her to whore for them. To... take men. One after the other. She was close to vomiting from the thought of it.

They'd left her with a bowl of something to eat and some water and then shut off the light, leaving her in pitch darkness. She'd decided right off the bat that it was better to appear meek and afraid.

So far it was working. They weren't being too rough. And they'd left her untied. That was a bad decision on their part.

She was afraid, that part was not an act. But meek? Hardly.

She used her hands to feel along the concrete floor. There was no way in hell she was going to eat the food they'd left but she needed the water. She was parched. She could tell she was dangerously dehydrated, especially after her parents had trapped her for so long.

Unfortunately, that was the least of her worries.

She was an idiot. She had got herself into this mess, and now she needed to get herself out of it.

It had been the third place she went to looking for work. The first place that hadn't cared that she'd lost her ID and didn't have references. But the joke was on her. If only there were anything funny about it.

The ad she'd found for body work had been a scam. They were running a brothel here, and from what she could tell at least 75% of the girls were unwilling participants in the scheme. She'd met a few of them before she was tossed into this dank room all by herself.

Their accents told her they were from all over the world. Their eyes told her they were beaten and broken. Like her, they were the disenfranchised. No one loved them.

No one would come looking for them.

But she vowed she would make sure this place got raided, the second she got away. These other women weren't going to be trapped here. Not if she had anything to say about it.

She closed her eyes, berating herself for the hundredth time.

How could she be so dumb?

When she'd walked in the place they'd taken one look at her and seen a gold mine. They'd drugged her. They tried to get her to put on some sleazy lingerie. She'd fought them tooth and nail when she woke but in the end they'd won, holding a cloth over her mouth until she stopped struggling.

When she came to the second time she was dressed in a black satin corset with lace panties, thigh high stockings and black heels.

How anyone could walk in those heels was a mystery. She could, but only because she was a dancer. And now, they'd given her a weapon.

Leaving her the heels was an oversight on their part. If anyone tried to touch her, she was going to stab them with those 4 inch stilettos. She would have already but she'd eaten a few bites of the food they'd brought the first time. It was risky but she'd been so hungry at that point she hadn't cared.

Mistake. Big mistake.

It had been drugged, sending her into a stupor yet again. She'd spent half the day in a dream state, with images from her past and present intertwining.

When she woke up her purse was gone. Not that she had anything in it. Her parents had taken her phone and her wallet.

She knew she couldn't blame them for this mess though. This was all her. Stupid and impulsive as usual. And now look at the situation she was in.

She would not give in. She would not let them force her to do one damn thing!

She wiped tears off her cheeks. At least they hadn't tried to turn her out yet. Soon though. She knew it was coming soon. She'd overheard them saying something about breaking her in before shipping her overseas.

They put girls as far away from the people they knew as possible. Foreign girls came here, American girls went- well, everywhere from what she had overheard.

She knew if that happened she'd disappear forever. She'd never see Kaylie again.

*Or Jack.*

The thought sent a spiral of pain through her chest. Even if he didn't want her, she'd still like to see him now and then. Even if they didn't speak. Just his presence made her feel safe. Just his *existence.*

*The world was a better place with Jack in it.*

She conjured up an image of him. She'd been doing this for almost a week now, ever since she'd been locked in her room and then this hole. It gave her plenty of time to think… to fantasize.

Mostly about Jack.

She imagined what he would do if he found her in this situation. As usual, he was staring at her disapprovingly. He'd be the first one to tell her she was an idiot for getting herself in this situation.

Of course, he wouldn't actually say it. He'd just project it with those steely dark eyes of his. And then he'd smile the teeniest bit, letting her know he was glad she was okay.

Janet moved back into the corner and held a shoe in each hand.

She knew what Jack would expect her to do.

She was going to fight.

# CHAPTER THIRTY-ONE

## JACK

Jack didn't even bother with the first two names on the list. It was getting to be late at night already and he knew the legitimate businesses would be closed.

But not the Body Work Special.

Christ, if she was in there, God knew what they'd done to her.

He would kill them if they hurt her. He'd kill them if they even touched her. He was pretty much ready to kill anyone who touched her.

She was his. They both knew it. And he was done fighting it.

Now he was just fighting to get her back. And once he did, he was keeping her. Didn't matter that she was too good for him. He would just have to learn to be good enough for *her*.

He texted Dev on the way. He told him to bring some guys in as few words as possible. He might need the backup. He didn't care if he made it out of there alive, but if anything happened to Janet, he'd lose his mind. Maybe permanently.

This was going to take some finessing. The Rub N' Tug was run by a rival gang. Nowhere as big as the SOS but twice as mean.

*The Viper's Disciples.*

He couldn't wait for the guys. If there was a chance he could stop them before they... he gritted his teeth, trying not to imagine Janet lying helpless underneath a paying customer.

He pushed open the glass door and walked in.

# CHAPTER THIRTY-TWO

## JANET

T*HUNK*

Janet's eyes fluttered open, only to close again. Was someone here? No... she'd dropped her shoe.

*Her weapon.*

She struggled to wake up as the realization sunk in: they'd must have drugged the water too. How could she fight them when they kept her drugged constantly?

She felt as if she were moving through molasses as she reached for her stiletto heel. She nearly tipped over but after three tries she had it firmly gripped in her palm.

*Fight Janet. No matter what. You fight.*

There was something happening outside the dark room, the 5 by 8 foot cage that had become her world. Loud voices, a gunshot, screams. Through her haze she merely acknowledged that there was a new development.

The question was, could she use it to her advantage?

She forced her wayward mind to focus briefly. Maybe... maybe she could use the diversion to escape. Get out. Run.

The darkest part of her asked where she would go... there wasn't anyone who wanted her around. Kaylie was her true friend but she still lived at home. Janet tried to think of a place to run to.

The only place she could think of was the clubhouse.

That's where Jack would be. Maybe he would know a place for her to hide. If he could pull himself off of the sleazy blond he'd been with.

But he would help her anyway. He had to. He cared, at least a little bit.

Didn't he?

But he was with her. The faceless girl he'd wrapped his arm around. She shook her head. That bastard had literally tossed her aside without a second thought.

The fury that thought engendered snapped her out of her stupor. She still felt slow, she still felt weak, but she was fighting it.

And she was winning.

If only so she could slap Jack's face when she saw him again.

# CHAPTER THIRTY-THREE

## JACK

Jack stared into the terrified eyes of the woman at the front desk. She looked like an aging stripper. He didn't respond to her chirpy greeting and offer for him to peruse the menu of options.

He simply said one word.

*"Red."*

The woman blanched and reached for a hidden button. Jack was on her in a second, lifting her in the air by her neck. He'd never hurt a woman, but right now he wanted to tear this bitch's head off.

His voice was low and vicious when he spoke.

*"WHERE. IS. THE. REDHEAD."*

The woman's eyes darted to the hallway behind him. He lowered her and released her throat just enough to allow her to gasp in some air.

"She's- in- the- back. Down the stairs and to the left."

He cursed. The basement. It sounded like a death trap. Once he got her, how the hell was he supposed to get her back out?

"What you need, bro'?"

He turned to see Dev and eight of the Spawn's behind him. He almost smiled at them, he was so Goddamned relieved to see them.

"They have Janet. She's in the basement. Make sure everyone stays quiet."

Dev nodded and gestured to Mike, the prospect. He stepped forward and started tying up the hostess. Jack sneered at her as he passed. What kind of woman did this to her own sex?

She was a fucking cannibal.

He stormed down the hallway, leaving it to Dev and the other Spawn's to watch his back. He didn't care one way or the other. He just had to find her.

He pushed open door after door until he came to the stairwell at the end of the hallway. He interrupted several paying clients getting their rocks off. He didn't care. They should be fucking ashamed of taking advantage of these women.

Janet was one of them. They might have used her like that.

He couldn't hold it back any longer. He screamed.

"JANET!!!"

Everybody stopped at the guttural bellow that emanated from his gut. For a long moment everything seemed to be frozen in time while they all waited expectantly to hear her reply. It was completely silent in the low lit hallway.

Until the world exploded.

Vipers seemed to be coming out of the walls. They had guns. They had knives. They had fists.

But they never got the chance to use them. Jack used his fists to fight his way through ten of them in seconds.

The Viking was in full effect.

# CHAPTER THIRTY-FOUR

## JANET

Janet heard the commotion upstairs. She waited, forcing herself into a state of readiness. Or almost readiness.

However ready you could be when someone had slipped you a mickey.

She swayed on her haunches, clutching a shoe in each fist. She wasn't going down without a fight. Her eyes closed sleepily and she forced them open again.

Footsteps. Heavy, loud. Running down the stairs. Toward her.

She lifted her body, ready to spring.

The doorknob turned without opening. Someone cursed outside the door. Then it was quiet.

"Get back!"

Was someone telling her to get back? She frowned in confusion and then decided to move back anyway. That didn't make a lot of sense to her, but she did it anyway.

*BAM*

*BAM*

*BAM*

The door burst inward with tremendous force, shattering the lock. Splintered wood flew everywhere but Janet didn't notice. She only knew that they'd come for her. It was time to fight. She leapt onto the intruders back and started slamming her heel into his shoulders.

Except she couldn't seem to stab him with it. The heels kept sliding off the leather.

The leather jacket.

*The motorcycle jacket.*

"Jesus, woman!"

She slid off him onto rubbery legs. The world started spinning as he turned to look at her. His huge hands gripped her shoulders.

"Janet baby? Are you alright?"

It was Jack.

"You came for me."

He nodded once, his hand sliding over her cheek.

"Yes baby. I came for you."

She wasn't sure if she was dreaming or not but either way she was extremely glad to see him. She smiled at him wobbily as she slid to the floor.

"Hi Jack."

He cursed and lifted her up.

"Are you on something, Janet?"

"Oh yes. Lots of things. Water. They put something in the water"

She was babbling as he carried her out of the place. She saw familiar faces in the periphery. There were Spawns everywhere. Devlin was here. But none of her attackers.

She let her head fall back onto his shoulder.

"Did they hurt you?"

"No. But if they tried I was going to stab them with my shoe."

He glanced down at her, clearly remembering that she'd attacked with the same shoe.

"Yeah, I noticed that."

She giggled at the disgruntled expression on his face.

"I still want to stab them for making me wear this trashy lingerie."

She closed her eyes and dozed off. But not before she caught the startled expression on his face as he finally took in what she was wearing.

Jack's eyes had never looked bigger.

# CHAPTER THIRTY-FIVE

## JACK

**H**e had her. He had his woman.

Out. They were out. She was okay. Hell, she was better than okay. They must have given her some sort of happy pill. She sure did look glad to see him though.

He raised an eyebrow as he stared down at her body in that get up.

Trashy, maybe. Off the charts hot? Definitely.

He realized they had an audience and he hastily tried to cover her up with his jacket. He had to put her down to get it off though. So far, she wasn't cooperating with his plan.

"Can you stand?"

She opened one eye and looked at him.

"No."

She closed her eye again, snuggling into his chest. Perfect.

Dev came over and slapped his shoulder.

"We better get out of here before the rest of the Vipers show up, man. She okay?"

Jack nodded and wondered how the hell he was going to get her out of here. Then in a flash of pure brilliance he figured it out.

"Dev, I need the cabin."

Devlin looked surprised but he answered without hesitation.

"No problem, man. It's yours."

"And your car."

Dev cocked an eyebrow at him.

"Can't ride with her in this state."

Dev grinned and chucked him the keys. Jack managed to catch them without dropping Janet.

"Actually, could you open the door for me? I kind of have my hands full."

He gestured to the passed out woman in his arms. Devlin grinned and took the keys back, opening the passenger side door. Jack carefully placed Janet in the seat and strapped her in.

He turned to see 8 different Spawn's staring at him with identical expressions of shock. He frowned at them fiercely and they all scattered, hopping on their bikes.

But he wasn't really mad. He was elated.

She was okay.

They hadn't hurt her.

She was safe.

Devlin smiled and shook his head, climbing onto Jack's bike.

"Always wanted to ride this thing man. Have fun at the cabin."

# CHAPTER THIRTY-SIX

## JACK

J anet's eyes fluttered open. She was in an unfamiliar place. Not the basement anymore. Not in her locked room, either.

*Where?*

Sunlight came streaming in through a window. She could see tall trees outside and hear the tinkling chorus of song birds.

*Birds?*

Where the heck was she???

She sat up and swung her legs over the edge of the bed. She stood up gingerly, feeling incredibly stiff. That's when the smell hit her.

The delicious, wonderful, marvelous smell.

*Pancakes.*

There was a dresser with a mirror across the room. She hurried over to it and stared in shock at the wan looking young woman staring back at her. She was wearing a large black t-shirt and nothing else.

Not large. Humongous. Built for a giant. It hung down to her knees.

Was she dreaming when she'd imagined Jack and the Spawns? Was she still kidnapped? Or had Jack saved her?

And more importantly...

*Who had changed her out of that hooker outfit she'd been wearing?*

Her stomach gurgled and she tentatively peeked into the hallway. Might as well get this over with. If she'd been sold off, she'd have to confront her keeper sooner or later. If it was Jack, she had to face him too.

But first she wanted to eat. She wanted to eat a *horse*.

Well, one made out of tofu anyway.

She tiptoed through the house- it looked like more of a cabin actually- following her nose down the stairs toward the delicious smells in the kitchen.

There was an old 1950's mint green table and chairs in there. A huge stack of pancakes was on a plate in the center of the table, along with a plate of bacon, a bowl of fruit and a carton of OJ, two glasses, and two plates. One of the plates had been eaten on. And there was an empty coffee cup.

Oh dear God, she smelled fresh coffee. Good coffee too, not of that instant little individual brew cups.

She'd never smelled anything so good in her life.

She caught movement out of the corner of her eye and turned abruptly. Someone was coming in from the deck. Leaning on the door jamb and staring at her.

*Jack.*

Not kidnapped then. Rescued.

He didn't say anything at first. He just took a sip of his coffee. He looked like he'd just taken a shower. His button down shirt was open in the front and she could see...

*Oh dear lord.*

She could see his chest and stomach. Hard and lean, with the ridges of flesh covered in tats. She tore her eyes away from all that glorious man flesh to see the glint of humor in his eyes.

"Sit."

She sat. She sat down so fast that her teeth knocked together. He strolled over leisurely and picked up her plate. He piled on pancakes first, then turned to look at her.

"How long was I out?"

"Fifteen hours give or take. You're a vegetarian right?"

She nodded mutely. Jack was... talking. She had never heard him put that many words together in one sentence before.

"So, no bacon."

"No bacon."

He loaded her plate with fruit and set it down in front of her.

"Eat."

She just stared at him.

"You- did all this?"

He gave her a mildly exasperated look and poured syrup onto her steaming stack of pancakes.

"Eat, Janet."

She did. She put the first bite of pancake into her mouth and moaned in ecstasy. She hadn't had real food in- oh god, almost a week. She shoveled in a few more bites, stealing glances at the man who sat across from her, calmly sipping his coffee.

Then she noticed something.

He had a dishtowel thrown over his shoulder.

Jack, The Viking, had a Goddamn dishtowel thrown over his shoulder like a regular chef!

"How did you learn to cook?"

He stood up and grabbed the empty coffee cup, walking to the counter.

"Coffee?"

"Yes please."

He poured them each a cup from the ancient percolator. It smelled so good. He carried it back over to her and set it down. She grabbed it and inhaled deeply. She'd never wanted coffee so much in her life. She took a sip and moaned. She'd never tasted anything so good in her life, either.

She looked up at him, not sure what to say. Jack was standing there, looking at her. Really looking at her. Not scowling. Not running away.

*She'd never seen anything so good in her life.*

He looked so clean and good and strong. His long wet hair falling to his shoulders in waves. His tight jeans hugging that insanely beautiful body. His dark eyes watching her watch him.

That's when it hit her.

She was in love with him.

*Oh dear God, she was in love with the Viking.*

She would have run out of the room if she'd had the strength. This was not good. Not good at all. How could she fall in love with someone who wanted nothing to do with her?

She was an idiot, that's how.

She felt tears sting her eyes and bent forward, focusing on her food. She ate in silence for a few minutes, wishing the floor would open a large hole and swallow her up.

"Foster care."

She glanced up at him sharply.

"What?"

"You asked how I learned to cook. When I was six years old I got moved out of the orphanage into foster care."

Her mouth almost dropped open. Jack was talking to her. Jack was talking about *himself.*

"Mrs. McNealy. She was my first foster mother. I never understood why they called it that though. There was nothing nurturing about that woman. Unless she was nurturing a bottle."

Her stupor vanished suddenly. She tried to imagine Jack as a boy but it was impossible. He was so strong and tough.

"She started training me on the first day. There were a couple other kids there. We each had a duty. The girl who'd done the cooking had just left for another foster home so Mrs. McNealy decided to teach me."

"She- made you cook for her?"

He nodded.

"I cooked for all of them. Well, whatever scraps she decided to feed her wards on any given day. She might have been a mean old drunk but she liked a clean house."

"Oh God, Jack... I didn't realize you were an orphan. How long were you with her?"

He shrugged.

"A couple of years. Until the next foster house. And the next one. In retrospect, Mrs. McNealy wasn't so bad."

She took a deep breath, realizing what he was saying.

They'd hurt him.

She wanted to kill them for that. She snuck a glance at him. He was looking out the window. She realized he was letting her in, telling her something no one knew.

"You got away though."

He nodded.

"When I was 14. I'd been tinkering with stuff for years. Garbage I'd find lying around. You have no idea how much junk poor people keep in their back yards. It's like they are afraid to throw anything away. I'd found an ancient broken down Indian bike and been slowly fixing it when Norm wasn't around to stop me."

He looked at her and Janet's breath caught at the raw pain in his eyes.

"He was a real cold bastard. He killed a kid once. In front of me. Made me lie to the social worker and say it was an accident."

"What would he do if you didn't?"

He rolled his shoulder and turned slightly, letting his shirt slide off enough so she could see part of his back.

She gasped.

He was covered in a blanket of scars. Huge welts. Thick ugly lines with a wide end that reminded her of something.

She felt her insides twist into a knot.

It was a belt buckle. Someone had beaten Jack with a belt buckle.

"As soon as that bike turned over the first time I left, and I never looked back. I couldn't help the other kids. I couldn't do anything but run. I went back later and beat the hell out of him, but that's another story. Those kids though... I still don't know what happened to them."

She stared at the beautiful man sitting in front of her as he pulled his shirt back on. He went back to looking out the window.

"You helped me."

He grunted and stood.

"We got the other girls out too. Sent someone back Dev knows to shut it down for good. A fed."

"Good." She nodded to herself and said it again. "Good."

"I didn't..." He looked at her and then away, clearly struggling with what he was trying to say. His eyes met hers again as he continued. "Nothing happened with that girl. At the club."

Janet's mouth opened.

"Oh."

That's all he said about it. But she believed him. He ran his hands through his hair.

"Are you finished eating? I want to show you something."

He walked out of the kitchen door without waiting for an answer. Janet stood up and followed him onto the deck.

The house sat above a small mountain lake. There weren't any other houses out here. They were completely alone.

It was beautiful.

She felt Jack's hands on her shoulders and stared up at him as he slowly turned her around to face him. He was staring at her lips. He was going to kiss her!

He leaned down and whispered into her ear.

"Are you sure you're okay?"

She nodded.

He put his arms around her and smiled sweetly. His smile was gorgeous. He'd only ever smirked at her before, and his face had barely moved.

This was a bright, shining thing in the middle of his chiseled face. Jack wasn't just sexy and hard. He was freaking *beautiful*.

"Good."

And then he chucked her into the lake.

# CHAPTER THIRTY-SEVEN

## JACK

Jack watched as Janet came up sputtering.

He was ready to jump in at a moments notice if she needed help of course but she looked fine.

Pissed off, but fine.

He smiled to himself. He liked getting her riled up. And it meant that she was okay. Even if she'd been scared, even if her own family had treated her like an animal, she was okay.

"What the hell, Jack!"

He shrugged, liking the way the wet t-shirt clung to her curves as she bobbed up and down in the water. Hmmm... he'd have to get her out of that soon.

*Very soon.*

"Sorry. You smelled."

Her mouth opened and shut like a fish. He sure did get a kick out of shocking her. He grinned and started taking his clothes off.

She shut her mouth abruptly and looked at him with a very different look on her face.

A very *warm* look.

He shimmied his jeans down over his hips, kicking off his boots with them. She was trying to look anywhere but at him. He glanced down and saw his cock was already rising.

He was hard just like that.

And he hadn't even touched her.

He took a running leap into the water five feet from Janet. Just close enough to splash her.

He came up to catch her reaction but she was gone.

SPLASH

Water came flying at his head. She'd swum around him somehow and was pushing water at him with her forearms. Damn, she was really getting some good waves with that technique.

He was on her in an instant, grabbing her arms and holding them in the air while they both kicked their legs to stay afloat.

"Don't start something you can't finish, Red."

She was laughing until she finally caught the look in his eyes. He stared down at this beautiful girl and watched as her eyes changed from laughter to desire.

Just like his were doing.

For some mysterious reason she wanted him as badly as he wanted her. It probably wouldn't last. She was a rich girl after all. A good girl. Well, mostly good.

But he didn't care. If he could only have her for a little while, that would have to do. He would take what he could get.

He knew he'd want her forever.

He moaned and pulled her against him, crashing his lips into hers. He released her arms and held her head, angling it so he could kiss her deeper, harder. She made a sexy little sound of surrender as he plundered her mouth with everything he'd been holding back.

Then they started sinking.

She was laughing when she came up. But he didn't smile. He couldn't. All he could do was feel and want.

He propelled her backward through the water until her back was against the corner of the dock. He used one hand to hold her hips against his, pulling one leg up and around his waist.

"Unfff…"

He held them up with one hand on the edge of the dock and began again. He kissed her endlessly, nibbling her lips in between long bouts of deeply tonguing her sweet mouth. He finally lifted his head and pulled at her wet t-shirt.

"Take this off."

She shook her head.

"What if someone sees me?"

"*I* want to see you."

She ducked out from under his arms and swam toward the ladder.

"Come back here. Now."

He hardly recognized his own voice. He was practically growling at her. She shook her head and clambered up the ladder to the deck. He hoisted himself onto the dock and stood at the end, ten feet away from her.

Her eyes were wide as she stared between his legs at his cock. He was fully erect now and standing proud at nine thick inches. She didn't look scared though. She looked… intrigued.

He raised an eyebrow at her as she backed away from him playfully.

"That's my t-shirt and I want it back."

She smiled suddenly and ran toward the house.

"Then come and get it!"

# CHAPTER THIRTY-EIGHT

## JANET

Janet ran up the stairs and into the bedroom she'd woken up in. She heard him behind her, his wet feet slapping the stairs. Two at a time.

He was right behind her.

She climbed onto the bed and pulled the t-shirt off. As soon as he appeared in the doorway she chucked it at him. It hit him in the face. She stifled a giggle.

Her aim was better than she thought.

He pulled it off his face off and chucked it aside, staring at her naked body. Then he was on the bed. Then he was on top of her.

It happened so fast that she would have missed it if she blinked.

She moaned at the incredible feeling of his hot chest pressing into her breasts. He felt so strong and hard against her softness. Then he was kissing her again. So he still wanted her. Good. She wanted him too.

So much it hurt.

But there was more than just passion in the kiss. He was kissing her like he cared. As if it meant something.

His hands found her breasts and he lowered his head to them.

"Oh God, Red."

She gasped as arousal shot straight to her center, spreading out in every direction. He readjusted himself so he could rub his shaft against her apex. She moaned as he stimulated her there with his slowly rocking hips without inserting himself inside her.

Clearly he was not in a hurry, damn him.

She whimpered as he pulled her nipple into his mouth, tugging sharply. Her hips were moving of their own volition. She wanted him to hurry up. She wanted him inside her now.

*Right now.*

He chuckled low in his throat and moved down her body. Her fingers were in his hair. Oh god- he was going to-

His lips pressed against her bare pussy, kissing her softly. Then he pulled back and his tongue snaked out. Her whole body arched off the bed as he lapped up and down her center, never pressing inside.

He used one hand to hold her hips immobile and the other one moved above his mouth to find the sensitive nub. He started lightly circling his finger on her clit and she bucked against him.

*"Jack!"*

She felt him smiling against her as he continued his slow exploration of her body. Finally he picked up his pace as he worked her clit and slid his tongue inside her. They both moaned.

Then he started to fuck her with his tongue.

It was the most erotic thing she'd felt in her life.

"Oh my God!"

She was beside herself. It was so intimate what he was doing. Never mind *how* he was doing it. His face was right there, pressing up against her pussy.

And he was going to town.

He was licking her as if he was starving. As if it was his mission in life to slowly drive her insane. It was working. She'd been shocked at first but now- now she was too desperate to be embarrassed.

She was close. He seemed to know it too. But he didn't let her go over the edge. He just kept her there, aching for him.

She was gasping for air as he lifted his head slightly to look at her. Her eyes were half open, watching as Jack devoured her sex. He lowered his head again. This time she felt his tongue on her clit as he slid one finger inside her.

"Hmmmm…"

He was really enjoying this, a voice said in the back of her head. She tried to move her hips, to pull his finger deeper, make him move faster, but he just laughed again and pulled her clit into his mouth, flicking his tongue against it rapidly.

*"Oh!"*

He was murmuring something but she couldn't understand him. He slid a second finger inside her and she moaned. She wanted- she wanted-

She screamed as the climax hit her. Her body shuddered violently as the biggest orgasm she'd had in her life tore through her body. He didn't stop the staccato motion of his tongue. He didn't stop sliding his fingers in and out of her. He didn't stop-

*"Ahhh!"*

She was shaking as he finally lifted his head. What he'd just done to her was like nothing she'd ever experienced in her life. She expected him to look smug but instead he looked desperate with need.

He growled as he slid his body up against her until he reached her mouth. He kissed her softly, as she stared up at him. He looked like he was in pain.

"Janet… I want to…"

"Yes. Oh God, yes."

Relief flooded his features as she felt him position his shaft at her juncture. He felt hot and hard against her, like silk and steel. He braced himself above her and stared into her eyes as he pushed forward.

# CHAPTER THIRTY-NINE

## JACK

He *was in heaven.*

Jack grunted like an animal as her warm heat enveloped him. Just the tip though. It was going to take him a while to get all nine inches all the way inside.

If that was even possible. He was willing to try though. More than willing.

*Desperate.*

She was so tight... and wet... and she'd tasted so Goddamn sweet in his mouth. The taste of her had inflamed him to the point that it physically hurt to not be inside her. But he had to make sure she was ready.

He had to make sure she wanted him as badly as he wanted her. Or close. Very, close.

He held her gorgeous hip with one hand and started to make tiny thrusts. He knew he was larger than average. Never mind that he'd never been with a woman as small as Janet.

He'd only ever been with the sleazy sweetbutts who hung around the club, and not in years. None of them had ever complained about his size. But none of them were as delicate as Janet.

He didn't want to hurt her accidentally.

He closed his eyes, not wanting to think about that.

Not wanting to think about anything but the way she felt.

She was tiny but somehow her body was allowing him in a little deeper with every stroke. He was going slowly even though he wanted to unleash himself, to take her roughly until he poured himself into her.

Maybe someday. When she was used to him. Then he could really let go.

She was making tiny whimpering sounds beneath him, mewling like a little kitten. *Unnff... God she felt good.* Nothing in his worthless life had ever made him feel a tenth of this pleasure.

Not even close.

She clenched down on him as he was pulling out and he lost control for a split second, driving in as deep as he could go. Her walls stretched taut around him.

*"Yes, Jack! Yes!"*

He stared down at her, unsure. But it was written all over her face. She wanted what he wanted.

He moaned and started pumping his hips into her. His shaft was sliding in and out of her sweet pussy with ease now. With every stroke her walls massaged and squeezed him.

It wouldn't be long now.

He increased his tempo as he felt her body start to convulse beneath him. Her cries grew louder, spurring him on. He worked his cock inside her like a machine, pistoning in and out, harder and faster by the second.

Suddenly he stopped and pushed himself inside her as far as he could go.

His cock gave a mighty jump. He moaned as he felt his seed erupt from his head, filling her up. He thrust into her a few more times as her body pulled at him, sucking him deep again.

Then he collapsed.

*Jesus.*

If he'd known it could be like that, he would have taken her the first time he wanted to. That very first night at the club.

He would have done anything to be inside her.

He hoped she would let him do it again. And again. And again.

*What he'd really like is forever.*

He rolled off of her and pulled her into his arms, staring at the ceiling. She snuggled against his chest in a way that suggested there was no place else she'd rather be. He allowed himself the luxury of thinking- hoping- she might let him keep her.

She might stay.

A cool drop of water hit his chest.

*What the-*

He laid back again when he realized she was crying. She wasn't crying because of him, was she? He never wanted to make her cry again.

"What am I going to do Jack? I can't go home."

He squeezed her. Not crying because of him then. Good.

"I know."

"They don't love me."

"They are idiots."

"How do you know?"

"I met them."

"You did?"

"I went looking for you when Kaylie told me- look Red, I wouldn't have had to meet them. I knew they were idiots the second Kaylie told me what they had done."

"Why?"

"How could they do anything but cherish you?"

She sighed and her tears welled up again.

"Don't cry for them, Red."

"I'm not."

He raised an eyebrow at her and she nearly burst out laughing. He was almost offended by the look of shock her face at the discovery that he had a sense of humor after all. Instead he decided that it was time to make love to her again.

Before she changed her mind and didn't want him again.

But slower this time.

Much slower.

# CHAPTER FORTY

## JANET

"I want to see you dance."

Jack's voice was a low rumble in his chest. It practically vibrated her whole body. Janet was cuddled up in his lap on one of the deck chairs, watching the sun go down.

"You do?"

He lifted her up and set her on her feet, facing him. Then he sat back down again.

Her eyes widened as he stared at her expectantly.

"Really dance."

She inhaled and exhaled shakily.

"I haven't danced in so long, Jack."

"So?"

"There's no music."

He just waited. She felt so awkward in front of him suddenly. What if she wasn't any good at it anymore? What if he laughed at her.

She peeked at him shyly. He lifted the corner of his mouth the teeniest bit. For Jack, that was a pretty big smile.

"Please, Red."

"Okay."

She took a deep breath and moved back on the deck. She'd perform the part of Giselle when she reappears as a spirit to save her lover. Of course, she couldn't do it full out without toe shoes, but she could mark it out. She'd have to be careful on the wood deck.

She tuned out everything around her and heard the music in her head. She rose gracefully as the spirt of Giselle into a full arabesque, one leg pointing high in the sky behind her. Then she fell into the dance, abbreviating the turns and leaps but doing most of the footwork.

The dance was one of lost love and redemption. She felt all the emotions of the dance filling her up and spilling out as she spun in revoltade after revoltade, finally sinking to the ground as Giselle returned to her grave.

Janet lifted her head to see Jack watching her with tears in his eyes. He lifted his hands and clapped, slow and hard, until she ran into his arms. He pulled her into his lap and kissed her.

"You are so beautiful. How could anyone be so beautiful, Red?"

She snuggled deeper into his chest. She hadn't danced in so long. She'd been afraid to. But here and now, it had felt right somehow.

She felt wonderful. Everything in this moment was perfect. She'd never felt so safe and secure in her life. Until Jack's next words brought reality crashing back down on her.

"Let's go home."

She nodded sadly. If that's what he wanted, she would do it. If she had to face her folks, just to get her stuff, she would. Then she would find a place to crash.

If that's what Jack wanted, then it was the right thing.

She'd do anything for him at this point. The last thing she wanted was to leave this beautiful place... The place where she'd finally had Jack all to herself.

It wasn't just that she didn't want to go home.

She didn't have one.

# CHAPTER FORTY-ONE

## JACK

"It's okay, Red."

Jack pulled up to Janet's parents house. Her bedroom window was boarded over. Good. He hoped everyone knew why. Then the neighbors would know what sick people were living there.

"I don't want to go in there."

He turned to look at Janet. She looked so small all the sudden. Like a lost little girl. He tried to smile reassuringly.

"So don't. I'm just going to get some clothes for you. Though you do look pretty cute in my shirts."

"Oh."

"Did you think I would take you back here? After what they did?"

"I- I don't know what to think. Or expect."

He leaned forward and pressed his lips to her forehead.

"You can stay with me for as long as you want."

"I can?"

"You can stay forever, Red."

When he pulled back she was staring up at him with an odd look. He never seen that look in anyone's eyes before. It told him that he was the most important person in the world to her. He inhaled sharply. He felt important suddenly.

He felt like he mattered.

Then she blinked and it was gone.

Jack got out of the car and walked up to the front door, pounding it with his fist. It was early, just after dawn. He didn't care what time in the morning it was.

After a minute Janet's father opened the door. He was bleary eyed. Clearly he'd just been woken up.

Jack shouldered him out of the way and walked straight to Janet's bedroom. He found a duffle bag in the closet and started shoving clothes into it. He opened a drawer and grinned at all the frilly lady items inside. He emptied the entire drawer into the bag and then moved to the next drawer.

Then he looked at the hanging clothes. Janet sure had a lot of fancy stuff.

He was rummaging around for something else to put her clothes in when he saw her father standing hesitantly in the door.

"Is she alright?"

"I need another bag."

"I'll get one. Is she?"

He nodded brusquely and the man disappeared, coming back with a garment bag and another large suitcase. He helped Jack as he packed Janet's things.

In the end, Mr. Mahoney ended up carrying half of her stuff out to the car with Jack. He teared up when he saw Janet in the passenger seat.

"Thank God you are alright."

Janet didn't say anything as they loaded the car. She stared straight ahead until Jack was in the drivers seat. She glanced at him for reassurance. He nodded. Janet turned to her father.

"Goodbye, dad."

That was it. She turned away from the open window and Jack pulled away from the curb.

He'd never been so proud of anyone in his life.

# CHAPTER FORTY-TWO

## JANET

Janet stared out the window of the SUV at the huge metal sign that read 'JH Bikes.' It turned out that Jack owned his own custom bike shop. He'd said he was good at fixing things. How had she not known about that?

From the looks of it, business was booming.

"I live on the top floor. There's a couple of empty floors up there too. It's not much but-"

"Are you kidding? It's awesome."

He looked relieved. She was coming to realize that he did care what she thought. Very much so. She smiled and got out of the car.

"Jack!"

A couple of guys were in the shop working. They raised their hands in greeting, looking at Janet curiously. Jack scowled and grabbed her stuff. All of it.

She looked at his hand gripping her luggage. He could carry a lot with those huge hands.

That wasn't the only huge thing he had... she blushed, remembering making love with him that third and fourth time on the deck in the open air. He'd laid a blanket down on the hard wood and then he'd taken her twice.

Fast the first time and then slow the second. That was four times they'd done it in one night. She was a little bit sore to tell the truth. But she didn't care.

Not one bit.

She followed him through a large metal door to an industrial elevator. He pulled the gate down behind them and threw the lever, watching carefully as they rose three stories. There were a lot of empty floors.

"Who owns this place?"

He glanced over his shoulder at her.

"I do."

She raised her eyebrows and looked around.

"This elevator has a lot of possibilities."

He turned sharply and threw the lever. His mouth opened as he gathered her meaning. He took a deep breath and shook his head to clear it.

Was he blushing?

He started the elevator again.

"I'm going to remember that you said that."

She felt a funny little dip in her stomach at his words. They sounded like a promise.

The elevator stopped at the third floor and he raised the gate. Janet looked around in wonder. It was an enormous loft. The kind you saw in magazines about wealthy New York Artists.

It was clean and spartan, with very little furniture. There were a few things here and there, a table and chairs under a long bank of windows. Bookshelves.

Jack read books?

And there against the back wall was an enormous bed. It looked like a California King. Of course it was. A big man like him needed a big bed. It rested on some sort of platform built out of wood.

"We can get more stuff if you want. You can pick it out. Whatever you want."

She looked at him curiously. He'd set her bags down and was watching her carefully.

She ran her fingers over the back of a heavy wooden chair.

"It's beautiful Jack. I love the furniture. Where did you get all of this?"

"I made it."

She stared at him, momentarily dumbstruck. Then she smiled at him. He looked so serious and she wanted to make him smile again. His smile made him light up.

"Is there anything you can't do?"

He smiled. An adorably lop sided grin that softened his face. For a split second she saw the little boy toiling in the kitchen. Unloved and uncared for. Her heart broke a little bit.

And then he said something so sweet it made her heart melt.

"I can't dance."

She laughed. She couldn't help it. Then she saw the metal staircase leading upwards.

"What's that?"

He took her hand and led her towards it.

"Come on. I want to show you something."

# CHAPTER FORTY-THREE

## JACK

Jack pushed open the door to the roof.

He'd only just begun building the deck up here in his spare time. But it was going to be spectacular when he finished. He stole a look at Janet to see what she thought.

"It's incredible!"

She was smiling and spinning in a circle.

"You can see the mountains from here!"

He walked over to a tarp and lifted it to reveal his tools.

"It's not done yet."

She was giving him an odd look suddenly. She looked… suspicious.

"How many girls have you brought up here, Jack?"

"None. Not ever. Listen, Red…"

She looked up at him.

"There hasn't been anyone in a long time. And before that it was just- once in a while."

"Really? But they must have offered…"

"No comment."

She giggled and hugged her chest with her arms. He stared at her long, beautiful legs. She was still wearing his t-shirt. He hoped she'd make a habit of wearing his shirts around the house. He took a deep breath and exhaled.

Here goes nothing.

Here goes everything.

"I want you."

She tossed her head in that familiar proud way. He grinned.

"You've already had me, remember? Four times."

She arched her eyebrow at him, daring him to answer that.

"No, Red. I mean I want you. Permanently."

Her eyes opened wide.

"You do?"

He nodded and smiled at her uncertainly, just a little bit worried about what she might say. That was a lie. He was a lot worried.

He was afraid.

She cocked her hip and gave him a sassy look.

"I thought you didn't do repeat customers."

"I never have before. I never… wanted to before."

She was beside him in an instant, laughing as she planted tiny kisses all over his face. He leaned down and took her lips. Ten minutes later he had a thought.

*They should finish unloading the car so he could take it back to Dev.*

His body molded itself to hers instinctively as she pressed herself into his with equal force.

Dev was going to have to wait.

# CHAPTER FORTY-FOUR

## DEVLIN

Devlin sat at the bar at the clubhouse, killing time before Kaylie got off of work. He spent a lot of time waiting on his woman these days. And he didn't mind a bit.

He waved as Jack walked into the room and crossed to the bar. He laid Dev's keys on the counter.

"Thanks."

"No problem man! I was psyched to try out your sick ride."

Donnie leaned on the bar and leered at them suggestively, handing Jack a ginger ale.

"Speaking of rides..."

He let the words hang suggestively, making Jack scowl furiously. Devlin couldn't help but laugh and slap Jack's back.

"How is Janet? Kaylie's been out of her mind with worry."

Dev and Donnie stared at Jack as a slow smile lit up his face. They'd never seen him smile that like before. Hell, they'd never seen him smile *period*.

"She's good."

"Good?"

He downed his ginger ale and nodded. Then he walked out of the clubhouse. An odd out of tune sound followed him as he left.

Dev glanced at Donnie who was staring at Jack with his mouth open.

"Dev, please tell me I've lost my mind..."

Devlin laughed at Donnie, who seemed to be at a loss for words for once in his life. He wished he had a camera to capture the awestruck look on Donahue's face. They were both in shock, but Dev had known his gigantic friend was hooked for a while.

The big guy was doomed, in the best possible way.

*"Is Jack humming?"*

"Yeah. That was definitely a hum."

"Any idea what song it was? I want to remember this moment perfectly."

"No clue. I don't think humans can hear that low."

Dev winked at Donnie and tipped back his drink.

"But Donnie?"

"Sup dude?"
*"You're next."*

TURN THE PAGE FOR SLADE, YOUR
BONUS SHORT STORY!

# SLADE

I may have sworn off groupies, but a man has needs. My surly next door neighbor is the first woman to get me going in years. Too bad she's playing hard to get.

JENNY

I've been hurt before. The safest thing to do is to hole up with my dog Basil in my grandmothers little cottage by the sea and bake my heart out.

When the obnoxious, **mega-rich rock star** starts building his house next door, I hate him on sight. For some perverse reason, Slade Kinney keeps trying to **charm his way into my pants.**

*Sorry honey, that's never going to happen.*

SLATE

I'm worshipped by millions. They scream my name and offer me anything I want. But I turn them all down. Until I meet her.

Jenny has her cute little sugar coated fingers wrapped around my heart. If I have to lower my guard completely to get her, I will.

---

This book was previously released under a different title. It has been extensively rewritten and expanded.

Enjoy!

Xoxox,

Joanna

# PROLOGUE

## SLADE

"Hey baby."

I barely glanced at the girl standing in the doorway, barely covered in a micro mini and corset. I got a vague impression of long blond hair and spiky high heels.

The dressing room was off limits. Invite only.

Especially for groupies.

"Not now."

She pouted. I didn't know her. As far as I knew anyway.

But I was never rude to women, even ones that didn't respect themselves. She looked like she was out of her element. Maybe even high.

I shook my head. It never ended. Rock had started off so exciting. I loved playing. I used to love the lifestyle.

But now I was sickened by the cheapness of it all. I had sworn off groupies almost a year ago. I just didn't have the taste for it anymore.

And I wasn't a cradle robber regardless.

"You want me to come back later?"

I sighed. I was tired. And the girl looked too young to be there. Lately I'd lost the desire for meaningless flings.

"No."

"Why not?"

"Sweetie, I think you are way too young to be here."

"Everything okay?"

Bruiser stood in the door behind her. He'd been with me forever. There was no one better at security. He kept everyone out, except cute chicks.

But that was more for the band than me.

Everyone knew I was over it.

"Bruiser, can you get her a ride home please. And give her a gift basket." I glanced at her dazed expression again. "Make sure she's okay. Give her some water, too."

"You got it boss."

He led the girl off and I sighed, staring into the mirror. Even without the after parties, I was toasted. Crunchy really.

I couldn't wait to get away from it all.

I knew just where to go, too. I'd just bought a plot of land in a quiet, seaside village on Long Island.

Peace and quiet. Just what the doctor ordered. Just one last sold out arena gig before I could get some me time. For once in my life, the entourage was not invited. I was going to unplug and unwind.

I rolled my shoulders and headed out to the stage.

*Showtime.*

# CHAPTER 1

## JENNY

*BANG BANG BANG BANG*
*Rattatat rattatat ratttat tat*

I pulled the covers over my head. Then I added a pillow, hoping that it would stop the incessant banging.

Nope.

Nothing I'd tried yet could block out the sound of the construction workers next door. Ear plugs. White noise machines. Sound canceling headphones.

They'd been building an enormous beach house next door for the past three months. With each nail, a little piece of my soul was getting smashed to pieces.

I lived in my Meemaw's house by the bay on the North Fork of Long Island. My grandmother had willed it to me, knowing that as a young chef, I would need a home after culinary school.

For the past two years, I had lived here full time, inspirited daily by my beautiful view of the bay, preparing my delicacies with sea breeze as my companion.

The breeze and my trusty sidekick, Basil.

But not any longer.

Not only was the new house disrupting my sleep but it would partially block my beautiful view to the South. It made me want to cry. In fact, I did cry about it. All the time.

I felt something cold and wet against my toe and peeked out of the blankets. Basil Rathbones was sitting by the bed, staring at me mournfully.

The dog had guilty expressions down pat.

"I know boy. You don't like it either."

I sighed and sat up.

"Oh well. We might as well get on with it."

I slid my toes into my slippers and padded into the kitchen to make coffee. I stretched my hamstrings and glutes while I waited for the coffee to brew. A plate of scones I'd baked the day before were sitting under a napkin. I selected one and dipped it into the coffee, taking a delicious bite.

As a pastry chef with my own small catering business, I was always baking.

And eating.

Basil was staring at me.

"What? I'll jog it off later."

He tilted his head to the side and whimpered. He wasn't buying it. I shrugged. A chef without a few extra pounds was highly suspicious if you asked me.

"Oh okay, you can have one too."

I reached into the old fashioned candy jar I kept on my tiny countertop and fished out a doggie scone. I made them twice a week just for my little fur buddy. They smelled kind of gross to me, but he loved them. Plus they were good for him.

That was extra important to me.

He was all I had since Meemaw passed.

Friends, sure. But family? Just this one scruffy little hairball. He was all I had in the whole wide world.

I sighed and rubbed his head while he finished his treat.

"Ready to go out?"

He whimpered and held his paw out.

"Alright buddy. Let's go. A promise is a promise."

I slipped into my jogging shorts and jog bra, throwing a worn in rock t-shirt over it. It was one I'd had since junior high school, with the neck and arms cut off. It had been washed a couple hundred times and as a result was super soft and barely covered my tummy.

I rubbed my belly contentedly. It swelled a bit, but I liked it. It kept me warm at night.

I laced up my beat up old sneakers and ran outside with Basil right at my heels.

It was a beautiful day. Clear blue skies with a couple of fluffy white clouds. A nice breeze. Warm but not too hot.

If I could ignore the sounds of construction from next door it would be one for the books.

*It was perfect.*

# CHAPTER 2

## SLADE

I*t was perfect.*

I stared out at the view. An unobstructed view of the calm waters of the bay. It was quiet here too, with only a handful of cottages dotting the shoreline.

This was the place I would write my next album in. Recover from the last tour and all the hard partying.

Regroup.

Lord knows I'd deserved it. I'd done everything the label wanted. The band. Our manager. Everyone.

Everyone except *me.*

I felt like I hardly ever did what *I* really wanted. Hell, I wasn't even sure I knew what that was. It was all about maintaining the image. Keeping everyone else happy.

As much as I loved the music, I had come to hate the other side of it.

Even the groupies were overly demanding. I'd done the whole Rock Star thing. Doling out one night stands like they were going out of style. Kept condoms in business for years. Even enjoyed it. A lot.

But now I just wanted some peace and quiet.

I wanted something real.

I wanted to be away from those people, if nothing else. The grabbers. The hanger ons. Everyone had a hand out. Everyone wanted something.

Even if it was just a ride on my cock, I was tired of it.

Too bad I'd had about three real friends in my life. And all of them from the South End of Boston where I'd grown up.

But they weren't exactly available for buddy time. They all had families of their own now.

Not like me, who still hadn't grown up.

Maybe I could tempt them down east with a little beach time at some point. All kids loved the beach, right? And I knew my buddies loved beer. I made sure to send them each a case from every country I toured in.

I'd found some delicious ginger beer in Japan with an owl on the top. A fucking owl. I tried to find the most outrageous names and flavors I could, plus some of the best. But mostly, the over the top ones.

That always gave them a laugh.

I'd already worked out at the gym today. I belonged to a very private facility in South Hampton, near where I was staying while they finished up the house.

That's about all I did really. Worked out, slept, watched TV. Had a few drinks.

It was heavenly.

Lonely as hell, but heavenly.

But soon. Very soon, I would be moving in. Next week actually. Then I could start over. Get settled. Create a home base.

Maybe even meet someone worth introducing the the southie crew.

I stared out the windows over the beach. I'd just met with the designer to approve the last of the plans. Everything was permitted, it was more about finishes now. Now I could just relax, check out the progress.

Take in the scenery.

Speaking of which… hello.

My eyes got wide as a gorgeous girl jogged by.

A really, *really* gorgeous girl with curves that wouldn't quit, a golden retriever and what looked like- yes- it was an ancient looking Ramones t-shirt.

And Chuck Taylor's.

Who the hell ran in Chucks?

Not to mention, the girl was bouncing out right out of her sports bra. I whistled to myself in appreciation. The girl was jiggling in all the right places.

Not just a little bit either.

I grinned. I just had to meet this girl. She had already run past the house. She had to come back this way didn't she?

I grabbed a bottle of water and strolled outside to casually 'bump into' her.

I watched her juicy bottom bounce out of view.

It was fine.

I could wait.

# CHAPTER 3

## JENNY

"Those are terrible for your arches you know."

I looked back over my shoulder. I'd been stretching my hamstrings when someone came up behind me.

I glared over my shoulder at the annoying stranger.

The very, very good looking stranger.

I stared at him. He had a chiseled face, wavy brown hair and a body that looked like it was straight out of a mens magazine.

Devastatingly handsome, really.

There was something familiar about him…

And smug.

My hackles started to rise.

I hated smug.

"What?"

"Your sneakers. They are terrible for your feet."

I glanced down at my shoes and then over at his.

He wore leather boots, expensive looking jeans, a soft black t-shirt and a leather jacket. And aviators.

So I couldn't see his eyes to see if he was being a prick or not.

I shrugged defensively.

"I tend to just use what I've got."

"Ah, so not a mindless consumer."

I stared at him, surprised.

"Yeah, exactly."

"I'm Slade."

He reached out his hand. His very large, tan hand. I took it, not really having another choice in the matter.

"Jenny."

He held my hand for a beat too long. He smiled at me warmly, finally releasing my hand.

"And who is this?"

He knelt down and shook paws with Basil. Basil responded by giving a loud yip and trying to lick Slade's face. I frowned. Basil didn't usually do that. He was usually as standoffish as I was.

Basil and I did not like strangers.

Maybe he liked the smell of money. It was practically wafting off the guy. Douchery squared.

Slade stood up again. I couldn't help but notice how fit he was. His shoulders were enormous, his stomach flat, and those legs... well, he looked a bit like a soccer player.

He probably had a great ass.

Not that it mattered. I had other things to worry about after all. Like an order of cookies for a birthday party, to be delivered later today.

"I have to get going. Come on, Basil."

"It was nice meeting you Jenny."

I gave him a half hearted wave and Basil whined, clearly not finished mauling the man.

I had to tug the stupid dog away with his leash.

He gave me a doleful look as I opened the front door. I just shook my head.

*"Traitor."*

But I gave him a treat anyway.

Then I washed up and got to work.

# CHAPTER 4

## SLADE

That is poetry in motion right there.

I watched Jenny jog away, practically drooling. She wasn't the friendliest little thing in the world, but looking like that, I wasn't so sure I blamed her.

She probably spent half her time beating off men with a stick.

My eyes widened appreciatively as her round little bottom flexed in those tiny shorts. Her long toned legs seemed to literally eat the ground as she ran. She looked graceful and determined, if a little curvy to make jogging practical. Her long honey colored hair swooshed back and forth against her back.

But it was her face that had startled the hell out of me. She was stunning. Not just beautiful. Certainly not just pretty.

No, Jenny was drop dead gorgeous.

High cheekbones, a strong jaw, stubborn little chin, pert delicate nose and the most luscious looking lips I'd seen in my life. And huge grey green eyes that completely dominated her face.

Hooded eyes that said 'keep your distance.' Her thick, sooty lashes and high arched brows framed a face that would stop traffic from fifty feet.

Jenny had a classic beauty that was impossible to hide, no matter how hard she tried to dress it down. And she did try to hide it, I could tell. She was unlike any of the many exceptionally good looking women I'd known over the years. Women who primped and preened themselves within an inch of their life.

This girl put them all to shame and she wasn't even trying.

Good lord.

I had a strong feeling I knew what I would be thinking about for the rest of the day. And the night. I reached down and adjusted myself.

I was getting hard just thinking about the girl.

That's when I noticed where she was going. She was turning into the ramshackle little beach hut that was right next door to my house.

In fact, it was so close I'd thought about trying to buy it. Make it into a guest house or something, or tear it down completely. But my lawyer hadn't had any luck so I'd let it go.

*Oh boy.*

With Jenny as a neighbor I was sure to have a lot of sleepless nights. That would be fine, as long as she joined me.

I smiled, feeling optimistic for the first time in forever.

I could think of a lot of interesting things to do with little miss hot pants in the dead of night.

# CHAPTER 5

## JENNY

A long, yawn and a stretch started my day. I rolled over and stared at the clock. It flashed at me a lovely, lazy day number. A number I hadn't woken to in months.

*10:08 AM*

I blinked and pulled out my ear plugs.

Blissful silence.

I sat up and looked around. Basil was on his back in a patch on sunshine, sound asleep. He snorted and his little paws jerked in the air.

"Is it Sunday?"

Ever since the construction had started I'd gotten one day of silence a week. Sunday. But today was Friday.

*Oh my God.*

It was quiet outside.

Was there a power outage?

*Was it finally over???*

I rolled to my feet and stood up. Basil huffed and didn't move. I almost laughed. My dog was like I was, a light sleeper. And for once, he was asleep past the crack of dawn.

For the first time in forever, I felt well rested.

I pulled on a pair of jeans and a t-shirt and made myself a small pot of coffee. I had orders to fill for the weekend so I got to work immediately after taking the pup out for a walk.

For a new small business owner like me, I worked 24/7, just to break even. But I loved what I did. Besides, business was picking up. Word of mouth about my recipes and magic fingers was spreading quickly.

Next year, I'd be flush.

Hopefully anyway.

I was dusting a mocha crumb cake with powdered sugar when the knock came at the door. I jumped a mile high and ended up covered with a film of powdered sugar. I cursed under my breath.

I didn't like unexpected visitors.

I especially didn't like them when I was working.

Oh well, it wasn't the first time I'd been covered in powdered sugar.

I set dow my accoutresments and went to answer the door.

Of course. It was *him.*

The slick, handsome stranger I'd met last week on the beach.

The one I hadn't been able to get out of my head.

It was twisted but whenever I had a quiet moment I found myself wondering about him, if I'd ever see him again. And promptly got pissed at myself for doing it.

*Slade.*

What a ridiculous name.

Yet somehow, it suited him.

I opened the door and stared at him through the screen door. He was wearing that same leather jacket and tight jeans. He leaned against the side of the door smiling at me, looking utterly at home.

He looked thrilled to see me, truth be known.

"Hi."

"Hey Jenny. Oh my god it smells good in there."

*I shouldn't invite him in, I shouldn't invite him in, I shouldn't invite him in.*

"Would you like to come in?"

"That would be great, thanks."

I opened the screen door, feeling a bit like I was in one of those scary movies. One of the ones where the heroine just invited a vampire inside her house. I almost laughed. Now he was going to either seduce me or suck out all my blood.

Maybe both.

He ducked under the door and stepped inside. He was so tall that he literally had to duck. The old cottage was built in the 1940's, where people had apparently been smaller than the ginormous man.

More like me.

Immediately Basil came over to say hello. They greeted each other like old friends, which I found annoying for some indefinable reason.

*Really annoying.*

He glanced at me and walked toward the kitchen. Not that it was far in the tiny beach house. But it was obvious he was intrigued by the set up.

"So, you are a baker?"

I nodded and crossed my arms over my chest. I'd forgotten to put on a bra and suddenly I felt naked. Exposed.

*Way to go, Jennster.*

The man was so damn virile that he made me feel tiny, weak.

Turned on as hell, which *also* annoyed me.

He grinned at me. The man seemed to be determined to wear me down. For some reason I found it enraging.

Mostly because it was starting to work.

"I'll have to buy a cake then."

"Sure. I can give you my menu or you can request something custom. I'm flexible."

He grinned wider, like I'd made a dirty joke. I groaned and turned away, riffling through the drawer for a menu. I found a relatively uncrumpled one and handed it to him. He was still grinning, damn him.

I just knew he was taking my statement as some sort of sexual innuendo.

*Ugh.*

"Thanks."

I shrugged and crossed my arms again. Had his eyes just skimmed over my tits or was I insane? It was impossible to tell through his sun glasses.

*What kind of D-bag wore sunglasses inside?*

"I'm glad you guys were in. The whole day has been madness really but I wanted to make sure I stopped by."

I cocked my head. What the hell was he talking about? He might be pretty, but I was starting to wonder if he was just a walking gonad.

"Oh?"

"Well, my big housewarming party is tomorrow night. I would love it if you came."

My jaw dropped.

*"Housewarming?"*

"Yeah, my house is finally done."

I was glaring at him, steam ready to come out of my ears. The daft man didn't seem to notice.

*"Which house?"*

He pointed out the window at the monstrosity next door.

"You are- the one who has been making all that noise for months now? You are the one who has destroyed my view?"

He looked a little bit alarmed as I stood up straight and pointed my finger at his chest accusingly. He held up his hands and backed away.

"Hey, I'm sorry it was loud or spoiling your view. I had no idea."

I scowled at him.

"Of course you didn't! Because rich, d-bags like you never. Ever. Think. About anyone else!"

He was smiling at me now, like I was amusing. Like I was a puppy biting his sneaker. I was not a puppy dammit!

"You and your construction crew have ruined my life for months! I've barely been able to think straight!"

His hands were high in the air like it was a hold up. Hell, maybe it was. I sure as shit wished I had a gun at the moment. He was lucky I didn't.

I definitely would have shot his cute little ass.

"Who are you anyway? Some slick investment banker? You are just the kind of person who is ruining this town!"

I yanked the menu out of his hands.

"I will not be baking you *anything*! Ever!"

He stopped backing away.

"The *kind* of people? Isn't that a bit prejudiced?"

I snorted. He was not leaving fast enough.

"What, scummy wall street guys are a protected class now?"

"I'm not a wall street guy. I'm a musician."

He pulled his sun glasses off and my jaw dropped. Huge golden brown eyes stared at me. I hadn't been wrong about the gorgeous part. I'd just understated it.

The man was a greek god.

Now I recognized him. I must be an idiot for not catching that before. He was one of the most famous men in the entire world.

*Slade Fucking Kinney.*

Rock Star and scumbag extraordinaire. Dater of models and actresses. Partier. Womanizer. Scoundrel.

And now he was here, ruining my view and trying to get into my pants to boot!

*Fanfuckingtastic.*

He had an earnest look on his face.

"Hey Jenny, ease up. I'm not the enemy I swear."

I crossed my arms again and sighed.

"Are you going to start throwing loud parties every night?"

"What? No. Just this one. It won't even be loud. I promise. I came out here to get away from all that bullshit."

I frowned and looked at him, saying nothing.

A famous asshole had just moved in next door. My peaceful, bucolic life was over as I knew it. My family had lived out here for three generations and now it was as bad as Brooklyn or LA.

The cute little stretch of bay had just officially become part of the hamptons, with a capital H.

*UGH.*

And to add insult to injury, for some bizarre reason I found him attractive.

Really, really attractive.

I even liked his music. In fact, if he looked at my collection, he'd see not only his latest album, but a few of the old ones. Including his first.

Not that I listened to music much anymore. The sound of the ocean was the perfect backdrop to- well, anything.

But I didn't want him to see his disks in my collection. Ever. Even if they were gathering dust.

*Goddamn It.*

Well, I just had to get him out of here before he noticed that was all.

"Fine. Here. Take the menu. Have a cranberry scone."

I thrust the menu into his hand and handed him a pastry I'd been experimenting with.

"Thanks."

He looked utterly baffled as I hustled him toward the door.

"So you'll come? Tomorrow?"

"Uh huh. Sure. Whatever. No problem."

He was grinning at me as I shoved him out the door. The poor man seemed a little slow witted to be honest. Maybe all that loud music and partying had ruined his brain.

Or he just really liked me for some obscure reason.

"Awesome! Come by around six. Or anytime really. Stop by whenever you want. If you run out of sugar, or you want to talk."

He grinned at me and it was like the sun came out. His teeth were perfect.

"Looks like you might need some more."

His finger brushed my cheek and he popped it into his mouth. My jaw dropped open. The sugar! This entire time I'd been coated in it.

I wanted to sink into the ground and disappear.

"See you later, neighbor. Oh, and thanks for the scone."

He smirked at me and bit into it before walking away. I stood behind the screen door, watching him. He looked back over his shoulder and shouted through a mouthful of crumbs.

"Delicious!"

I shut the door rapidly and leaned against it.

Had I just agreed to go to his stupid party? I could always bail on it, I reasoned. It was doubtful he would notice if I wasn't there.

He'd probably make it a habit of stopping by though. I groaned. I'd just have to be firm with him. Rude even.

Lord knows I was good at that.

At least he was gone now and I could hide the damn CD's!

# CHAPTER 6

## SLADE

F*ucking A, that was tasty.*

I licked the last of the crumbs off my fingers. I'd much rather be licking my delicious, if cantankerous neighbor though.

*Head to toe.*

She'd been covered in sugar and almost certainly not wearing a bra. I'd been aroused from the moment I set foot in her house.

Hell, I'd been aroused since the moment I met her.

I glanced at the menu and smirked.

Her company was called Jenny Cakes. How cute. I'd definitely like to do something with her cakes…

Lots of filthy, dirty things.

I had a feeling she had never met anyone quite as creative as me.

The best part of it was that her phone number was on the menu. It was a cell obviously. So I could text her.

I was going to break down her defenses one by one. Little miss Jenny Cakes had no clue what was coming for her. I could be very determined.

It wasn't by accident that I was one of the highest paid musicians in the world.

I'd start with dazzling her with the food and fine wines at the party. I'd make sure the whole thing was low key. I would prove to her that I would be a good neighbor to her.

Kind. Considerate. Attentive.

And more.

Much, much more.

For a moment I paused to wonder if it was just her obvious disdain that was making me so determined. But I didn't just want to get into my feisty neighbors jogging shorts. I wanted more.

The girl was not star struck in the least. That didn't happen to me too often. It was like going back in time to when I'd just been another guy in South Boston.

Actually, it never happened to me. This had not happened to me once, even before my first album dropped.

Oddly enough, I liked it.

But that wasn't the total reasoning for this absurd fascination. Obsession really.

I could clearly remember the shot of pure lust that had surged through me. It was an instant reaction. It started in the first moment I saw her.

That had been from a distance too. Up close she'd been far more devastating.

All before I realized what an adorable pain in the ass she was.

I laughed. Maybe that is what I liked the most about her. Jenny was real.

I waved at the crew that was unpacking and cleaning the house and headed into the office. I fired up the computer- the one thing I'd set up by myself. Then I started googling.

I wanted to know everything about Miss Delicious Cakes before I planned my attack.

And it would be an attack. A gentle one. But still.

I always played to win.

# CHAPTER 7

## JENNY

*Bzzzz bzzzz*

I groaned, trying to focus on the book in my lap and losing the battle. My phone buzzed for the third time. I knew who it was.

*Him.*

It was almost 7 pm. My new neighbor wanted to know when I was coming over.

*How about never?*

Still, the party did sound nice floating through the open kitchen window. People laughing, soft music playing. I could practically hear the champagne fizzing.

Thankfully it was not the raging drug fest I'd been afraid of. It was tempting to just go over, let my hair down for once. But I held firm.

Slade would never, ever leave me alone if I gave in now. Well, not until he moved on to the starlet du jour. Ugh, knowing you were going to get dumped before you even said yes to a first date was not cool.

I didn't like this feeling at all.

I gave up on the book and went back to the task waiting for me on the table. I leaned over my laptop, trying to stare the numbers on my spreadsheet into submission.

As a sole proprietor/independent contractor I was supposed to do my taxes on a quarterly basis. But I didn't have enough money for an accountant. So I'd gotten some fancy software program that I was still trying to figure out.

Technology was not my friend. I liked paper books, not ereaders. Phones and computers baffled me.

I didn't even belong to Facebook.

The bottom line was, I hadn't paid taxes for this year at all yet.

*Ugh.*

A soft rapping came from the front of the house. Basil sat up and started whining pitifully. I sighed.

Someone was at the door.

Obviously it was Slade. The man just would not take 'no' for an answer.

Annoyance shot through me, intermingled with something else.

*Anticipation.*

I hated myself for feeling it, but it was there. I hated liars. I never lied. Not even to myself.

Especially not to myself.

I sighed and went to answer the door. Sure enough Slade was standing outside with two glasses of champagne. As usual, he was smiling at me.

*What the hell did he have to be so damn happy about?*

Oh right. Being rich, famous, gorgeous and talented as hell was probably a lot more fun than being an awkward, chubby girl who liked to spend more time with flour and baking soda than other human beings.

"Hi Slade."

He gave me a charming look and made a scolding sound.

"Tsk tsk tsk. You promised."

"Sorry, I forgot. Paperwork. Really busy."

I brazenly tried to shut the door in his face. But he was too fast. It was almost like he knew what I was going to do before I did it.

He reached down and opened the screen door, inviting himself inside.

*Ugh, just come on in. Exactly like a vampire would. Once you let them in, you can never get rid of them.*

He glanced over at the stack of papers and receipts on my small dining room table. Which doubled as a desk. And tripled as a pie cooling rack. Or a place to roll out dough.

Every now and then I actually ate a meal there too.

"Come on doll, it's Saturday night. Have a glass of champagne. Loosen up."

If only he knew how much I hated people calling me pet names. Or telling me to loosen up. Or relax.

I didn't want to relax, dammit. I wanted to be tense. On my guard.

Relaxing was dangerous.

Sexy as hell men were dangerous.

Slade was extra, extra dangerous.

The last time I'd actually taken that advice, I'd gone down a pipeline that was impossible to resist. It had taken me years to clean up my life after the last lothario I'd let in. Jake had destroyed my peace of mind.

He'd nearly destroyed my life.

It was sure as shit not going to happen again.

Well, maybe just for one night... I could just go and come back. See how the other half lived. It's not like I had to sleep with him for real, was it?

I took the champagne and downed it, handing the glass back to him.

"Happy?"

He was staring at me as if he were star struck. Honestly, the man looked like he wanted to eat me alive. Or lick me anyway.

I wondered what he tasted like.

A funny feeling started to pool in my stomach.

Maybe I kind of wanted him to. Lick me, that is. I had a few ideas about where he could start...

*Ugh, no STOP IT JENNY.*

He smirked and handed me the other glass. I rolled my eyes and took it, taking a lady like sip. He laughed.

"Come on."

"What?"

He grabbed my hand.

"I'm taking you with me."

"But I'm not dressed!"

He didn't let go of my hand as he turned and looked me over. Thoroughly. Very thoroughly.

He seemed particularly intrigued by my feet.

I was barefoot in jeans and another old rock t-shirt. No bra. My hair was down and I wasn't wearing a stick of makeup.

Not that I ever really did. I liked a good lip gloss now and then. But I already attracted more attention than I wanted. Usually from guys who did not want a meaningful relationship, if you know I'm saying.

Makeup just made it worse.

Meanwhile *he* was wearing a very expensive looking button down shirt over another pair of soft looking tight jeans.

The man really knew how to wear jeans.

"You look perfect."

He let out a low whistle and started dragging me again.

"Wait!"

He sighed as if very put out and waited while I grabbed my keys and a cherry chapstick. He smirked at that. Then he took my hand and dragged me out of the house, sighing impatiently as I locked the door.

"Is that really necessary?"

"Well there are all sorts of strange men out tonight. So, yes."

"Touche."

He laughed again and threw his arm over my shoulder. For some reason he seemed to find me charming. No matter how hard I tried to put him off.

Maybe he was on drugs. He was a rock star after all. He *seemed* straight though.

And his big strong arm felt heavenly around my back. It had been a while since anyone hugged me, that was for sure.

It was kind of sad but the truth was, my only source of physical affection was a dog.

An awesome, off the charts amazing dog, but still.

"Come on doll. Let's get you some more of that champagne."

That's when I realized that he hadn't been wearing sunglasses for the first time. I was completely bamboozled by his stunning good looks.

His eyes. Good lord, those eyes.

They were brown. But that word didn't do it justice. They weren't chocolatey. They were amber.

Warm, glowing amber.

I let him lead me over to his house.

# CHAPTER 8

## SLADE

I sat in the low slung all weather couch on my deck. It formed a semi circle and was filled with people laughing and talking in front of an eco gas fireplace.

Soft music played, classics and songs from the 60's and 70's. It was comfortable, and surprisingly fun.

I didn't have anything against loud music. It just overpowered the sound of the ocean less than twenty feet away.

And according to Jenny, that would be a travesty.

I had to admit, I agreed with her.

She'd also programmed the music after I handed over my iPod.

Jenny was full of surprises as she sat beside me tonight.

The girl was not only relaxed, she was sparkling. She was surprisingly well read and sharp as a tack. There were revealing moments as well, like when she mentioned that she was well read only because she spent so much time alone.

I'd felt a strange hitch in my chest at the thought.

Then there was the time she'd said that she was alone in the world. Literally. She hadn't been throwing a pity party, on the converse, she'd made a joke about being an orphan.

Something about how simple the holidays were when you didn't have any living relatives. None worth mentioning anyway.

Everyone had laughed.

But it had broken my heart.

Just a little bit.

Just enough to crack it open and let something else in.

Everyone was drinking and relaxing but I'd switched to mineral water about a half an hour ago. As soon as the party started to thin out. I wanted to be relatively sober when I kissed her.

And I *was* going to kiss her.

Of that I had no doubt.

Kissing, and hopefully a whole lot more.

Now, I just had to keep her distracted while I hinted that everyone else should leave.

Jenny leaned back and closed her eyes, with no idea of what I was planning.

She wouldn't be so relaxed if she did know.

# CHAPTER 9

## JENNY

C*RACK*

My palms made contact with Slade's hands again. He was letting me win the game of slap, I had no doubt. But I couldn't stop laughing.

Besides, I figured he deserved a slap or two. Especially with the dirty looks he'd been throwing my way all night.

Not dirty.

Sultry. Hot.

*Smokin' hot.*

He'd been sitting next to me for most of the night, despite having thirty something other guests to attend to.

It was almost like he was afraid to let me out of his sight. Like he knew that I might sneak back home and he wouldn't get a chance to- well, I wasn't sure exactly what he was after. But I figured it included both of us, wearing as little clothing as possible.

The guy could have any number of gorgeous women at the party. I'd noticed his yoga teacher staring at him, throwing him hints all night. He ignored her completely.

For some reason, it seemed like he actually wanted *me.*

*And only me.*

I'd felt his eyes almost constantly. He'd managed to slide closer every half hour or so as well. Until his thigh was pressed against mine and his arms slung casually over the back of my seat.

He was marking his territory, no doubt about it.

It felt completely natural for some reason. Even though I knew he was putting the moves on me. He wasn't being overbearing but it sure as shit wasn't subtle either.

Now we were facing each other, two of the last people at the party. I kept getting up to leave but he kept pulling me back down and entertaining me with some other wild story.

He had lots of wild stories. And snacks. And fizzy, delicious beverages.

Now he was letting me slap the shit out of his hands.

*"Ow!"*

He winced and held his hand dramatically. I laughed giddily. I hadn't really hit him hard. Oddly enough, even after anonymously hating my neighbor for all this time, I didn't want to.

"You deserve it for waking me up all those mornings!"

"It wasn't me! If I had known I would have told them to start work at nine. No-ten!"

I laughed. It was impossible to stay angry at the man. He wasn't just devastatingly handsome, or rich, or talented.

He was funny as hell.

I harrumphed and nodded to him.

"Well, ten am is the perfect time to get out of bed."

His eyes warmed up and he leaned forward, stroking my cheek.

"Or get into it."

He was going to kiss me. I knew it. I hesitated for a moment and then turned away imperceptibly.

"I should go. Basil needs to go out."

"I'll come. We can try and finish some of this champagne."

I didn't say yes or no but when he followed me homeward, I couldn't wipe the smile off my face. Nobody had paid me this much attention in years. Mostly because I hid away from the world but-

*Now where had that come from?*

I loved my quiet little life. I was safe here. Nobody bothered me or made demands. Sure it got lonely sometimes but…

Aw, hell.

*It got lonely a lot.*

"Hey, Basil!"

Basil was ecstatic to see us as we came in the door. He grabbed his leash between his jaws and rolled onto his back, encouraging Slade to rub his belly.

It was a bonafide love fest.

Strangely, I felt left out.

"Alright, let's go you two."

Slade followed me to the beach, with Basil leading the way. I always leashed Basil, mostly for his own safety. I'd heard of dogs getting lost out here and didn't want to take a risk.

After all, Basil was all I had. Basil and a beach house. And my business, Jenny Cakes.

*Gee, that was depressing.*

I swigged deeply from the champagne bottle Slade kept handing me. They were laughing while Basil ran circles around us. Slade looked serious all the sudden as he reached out and grabbed my hand.

He rubbed his thumb over my palm and pulled me towards him. My laughter faded as I stared up at him. He was smiling softly as he looked hungrily at my lips.

He moved in. I moved away.

I took another swig and pulled free of his hands.

"Let's go swimming!"

His eyes lit up as I reached for my waistband, swiftly unbuttoning it and tugging down the zipper. His jaw dropped when shimmied my jeans off and ran into the water.

"Hey, wait for me!"

I turned back to see Slade stripping down to his undies and chasing me into the bay.

# CHAPTER 10

## SLADE

I was having the time of my life. No joke. It literally felt like the best time I'd had in my entire life.

*Because of her.*

There was no one on Earth like her. Jenny was so raw and present. So real. So free.

So intent on not letting me kiss her.

But if there was one thing I knew, it was that I was going to convince her otherwise.

Starting now.

We were swimming in the cool, easy waves that rolled into the bay. It was free from the dangerous undertow or rough currents that you faced on the ocean side. It was also a haven for biting flies and mosquitos.

Not that the real estate agent who'd sold me the lot even mentioned that.

But that made it safe for a midnight swim, even slightly inebriated. Which we both were.

Well, maybe more than just slightly.

I grinned as Jenny flipped over onto her back and stared at the sky. She couldn't know how entrancing her face looked, with just her nose, chin, forehead and lips visible above the surface.

Oh, and her breasts. It was hard not to be distracted by those glorious bouncing globes.

I licked my lips as her breasts bobbed against the waves. I was instantly hard, just like that. I almost had to shake myself to focus on what she was saying.

"There's no place like this on Earth."

"You're right."

"No place so beautiful. Or unspoiled."

I grinned and decided it was time to make my move.

"Especially now."

She turned to look at me as I rolled her to her feet. The bay was only four feet deep this close to shore. Deep enough to get wet, but hard to drown in.

Jenny was so tiny that the water reached up to her chest.

"What do you mean?"

I brushed my hand over her silky cheek. It was now or never.

*"Jenny…"*

The raw hunger in my voice was unmistakable. I lowered my lips to hers. I couldn't have stopped myself if I'd tried.

Not that I was trying.

Jenny felt, and tasted, incredible. She was a feast for my senses. In my hands. Under my mouth. Against my tongue. And when she opened her mouth to gasp in surprise I wasted no time.

I went for the gold.

My tongue danced inside teasingly to explore Jenny's delectable mouth. I swirled it against her delectable tongue. She stood stock still as I teased her mouth, begging her to kiss me back.

Once, twice… the third time her tongue responded to mine.

That was it.

*I was in.*

# CHAPTER 11

## JENNY

**W**as this really happening?

I moaned against Slade's mouth. His hands were everywhere under the water, inflaming me. He started stroking softly between my legs.

Even through my panties, it felt incredible.

How could I be so hot when I was submerged in the Atlantic Ocean?

Slade stopped kissing me long enough to tilt back slightly and lift me up. His lips and tongue seared the skin along my neck and collar bone.

He growled in frustration when he couldn't get at my breasts and set me back down.

He ran his thumb over my cheek and grabbed my hand.

"Come on."

I followed him back to the beach in a lust filled daze. He kissed me again and looked around, whistling for Basil. Slade scooped up the leash and led us both back toward my house.

I was as obedient as a well-trained dog.

I felt like I was in a champagne and kissing induced dream. But one thought kept pulsing through my mind. A thought that should have scared me. But it didn't.

*I was going to sleep with Slade Kinney.*

He opened the door. His damp hair fell over his forehead as he smiled at me. His hand felt warm on my back as he guided me inside.

At this point, the warning bells in my head went completely silent, overwhelmed by lust.

I would just sleep with him. Once. That would get him out of my system. Right? Yes, I told myself yes over and over again.

Then I could go back to my safe, boring little life.

But for now…

I stood in my living room, watching while Slade shut and locked the door behind him. Then he pulled me into his arms. His eyes were dark and hot and concerned.

"You're shaking."

He pulled my shirt up and over my head, casting it aside. I was naked now, except for my underpants. This was new. The lights weren't even dimmed. I'd spent every moment I'd ever been naked with a man trying to keep him from seeing me.

Slade looked. I could feel him looking. My skin pricked with heat as his eyes slid over my flesh.

But somehow he didn't make me feel exposed. He didn't stare, or ogle my large boobs. Instead he silently *appreciated* me. Just for a moment. Then he pulled me against him and kissed me again.

*Ohhh...*

He laughed a minute later, pulling away.

"We'll never get dry this way. Do you have a towel?"

I nodded and padded over to the linen closet. I turned expecting him to be watching me. Checking out my half naked ass. Instead, he'd followed me. He was inches away, his body giving off tremendous heat.

He pulled the towel out of my hands and started to dry me off. I gasped as the circulation rushed to my skin, warming me from the outside in.

It was the most sensual rub down of my life.

His hands skimmed my sensitive places as he patted and briskly rubbed me with the towel. He bent down to address my lower half and rolled my soaking wet panties down my legs. He didn't give me a chance to be shy. He wrapped the towel around my back and in the front-

In the front, he used his mouth the whisk the salt water away.

Gently, carefully, he tasted me.

Slade Kinney was eating me out while I stood in the hallway of my Gran's beach shack. And he was doing a damn good job of it too.

*Oh my god.*

His lips were soft against my pouty sex. He licked, teased and nuzzled me there, all the while making appreciative, sexy little noises.

Those noises alone were going to drive me insane. So was the way he was toying with me, never quite giving me what I wanted. What I wanted was more pressure, more contact, more speed.

*I wanted more. Now, dammit.*

But he just lazily traced the outline of my dewy slit with his tongue. Over and over again. Now and then he changed gears and flicked his tongue rapidly against my clitoris. Not enough to let me come. Never long enough to do more than turn up the dial on my arousal.

And I was already very, very aroused.

"Slade… Oh God, what are you doing to me?"

He chuckled and kept going as I gripped his shoulders and hung on for dear life.

"Please…"

He murmured something against my dripping petals. I tugged on his hair. I was close to begging.

"Slade!"

I expected him to come up with a smug grin on his face. Instead he came up looking serious. And as desperate as I felt.

"Bed. Now."

I nodded breathlessly and pointed toward my bedroom. He scooped me up like I was a skinny little thing. He carried me down that the hallway and kicked the door open, tossing me on the bed.

I watched in awe as he closed the door in a startled looking Basil's face.

Then he peeled his shorts off and climbed on top of me.

# CHAPTER 12

## SLADE

*P*lease give me the strength to do what I need to do.

The writing woman beneath me was going to drive me insane. Literally and completely insane. I felt like I was going to wake up in a mental institution, wrapped in a straight jacket.

I didn't mind though.

Jenny was worth it.

I'd never been this turned on in my life. Not even close. I held my breath as I lowered my body so that it pressed against hers.

*Dear Lord.*

She felt so good, the woman was giving me religion.

I kissed her again, unable to help myself no matter how badly I wanted to get on to the main event. My cock pressed tauntingly into her smooth belly, mere inches from where it wanted to be.

Buried deep inside her.

"Jenny? Do you have any protection?"

"What?"

"Do you have a condom?"

"I don't have any."

I groaned, my cock twitching in frustration. Neither one of us were in our right minds. I knew I was going to screw this woman senseless, condom be dammed.

"Oh God- Jenny- are you on the pill?"

She was staring up at me from beneath hooded lids.

"No. There hasn't been any reason to."

I moaned, realizing I'd been right. Jenny hadn't been with anyone in a long time. In some way, it felt like she'd been waiting for me.

Maybe I'd been waiting for her, too.

"Fuck- listen- I'm clean. I want to do this. We'll just be careful."

She nodded at me and I exhaled in relief. I'd been afraid she would tell me to go fuck myself. I wouldn't even blame her if she had.

"Christ- Jenny- I don't think I can wait."

"Uh huh."

"I can- I can pull out."

"Yes. Okay. Good idea."

I reached down and rubbed the tip of my swollen cock against her juicy little pussy lips. She whimpered in need. That was all it took.

The thin thread of control I had snapped.

"To hell with it."

I pushed forward, easing into her sweet little pussy. She was so tight that it felt like a fucking Boa Constrictor was strangling my unprotected cock. In a good way though.

A very, very good way.

"Unnnffffff…"

Her slick walls massaged my sensitive shaft as I inched forward. The girl was tiny to begin with, true, but I could tell she hadn't done this in even longer than I'd thought.

A long while.

Something about that made me even more excited if it were possible. She wanted me. After all this time, it was me who she'd allowed inside her.

Inside her, to heaven.

I grimaced and slid forward a bit more, being careful not to hurt her. She was so tiny, so tight, I knew my cock would hurt her if I let loose. So I kept myself in check, opening her, holding back from ramming into her the way I wanted to.

Not yet anyway.

But soon.

*Easy boy.*

I was about halfway inside her when I heard it. It was so faint, the softest of whispers. I froze, staring down at her beautiful face. She was breathing heavily, looking me straight in the eye.

"Please…"

"What is it Jenny?"

"Slade, would you please fuck me now?"

I groaned as my hips jerked involuntarily, sending my cock deeper into her sheath. She wrapped her long, silky legs around me.

That was it, I was gone.

*Game over.*

Long deep strokes that made my entire body flex as I pistoned my shaft in and out of her. Slow at first, but picking up steam until I was fucking her like a freight train. But still I held back.

At least until I felt her sugar walls start to undulate against me.

Jenny was coming. And it was a beautiful thing. A beautiful, insanely sexy thing.

"Oh oh oh!"

The feel of her combined with the sweet, sexy noises she made were too much. I lost it.

I was thrusting wildly into her when I felt my cock start to spurt. I moaned and tried to stop but I couldn't. There was no way in hell I was pulling out now. I literally couldn't.

We'd waited too long, gone too slow, I was coming inside her and there was nothing I could do about it. My shaft was pulsing hot slippery streams of come straight into her pussy.

"Ahhhh- fuck!"

I pinched the base of my cock and yanked free, covering her belly with my seed. I was still coming. At least I hadn't left it all inside her.

But I knew that plenty had ended up inside her. I'd had an unusually large load. Massive, really. More than enough to impregnate her.

*Much more.*

It had been a while for me too.

I gasped and rolled onto my back, stroking the last of my cum out into my hand. I grabbed some tissues and wiped her soft belly clean.

*Shit. Jenny is going to kill me.*

I was an idiot. I'd just blown the best thing I'd had in my life. A shot at something real.

Not that I minded the idea of getting this girl pregnant. I loved that idea. But I did mind the idea of possibly pissing her off enough that she might not want to do this again.

Because I wanted to do it again. A lot.

More than anything.

In fact, I was already getting hard again.

"Jenny?"

"Uh huh."

"Can we- do that again?"

"Uh huh."

Well then. I smiled and started kissing my way down her body. If I kept her turned on enough, and coming until dawn, maybe she'd forgive me for making a mess of things.

I'd do my best to make her want me back, for good.

# CHAPTER 13

## JENNY

O*h my.*

I stared at the ceiling, still trying to catch my breath. It was near dawn when we were finally finished with round three. That had been the marathon round, the long, slow fuck that would leave us both sore in the morning and for days to come.

I'd started out on top that time but by the end I was on my back. That had been a particularly interesting position, with my legs thrown over Slade's shoulders while he slowly ground his magnificent prick inside me.

And it was magnificent. Perfect. Beyond anything I'd imagined.

Slade had the blue whale of cocks. It was the eighth wonder of the world. It was a freaking skyscraper.

He'd been tireless, one hand gripping my hip while the other had danced lightly over my clitoris, sending me into orgasm after orgasm.

*Good lord, the man knew what he was doing.*

Finally we'd wound up tangled in the sheets, each feeling like a melted puddle of goo. There hadn't been much talking so far. There hadn't needed to be.

It was the best night of my life.

Too bad it could never happen again.

He was tracing his finger tips over my hip when I caught his eye.

"That was amazing."

He smiled at me tenderly.

"*You're* amazing Jenny."

"Slade- this was just what I needed. Thank you."

He laughed and kissed my neck.

"You make it sound like I did you a favor."

"You did. But it can never happen again."

*"What?"*

I'd stroked his cheek softly as my eyelids fluttered shut. I was nearly asleep. He sounded annoyed. I felt him sit up in bed beside me.

But it didn't matter. I meant it. I wasn't going to open myself up to a fling with him, no matter how tempting it might be.

I had to protect myself better than that.

"Just this one time. Thanks for making it count…"

Then I rolled over and went to sleep.

A soft tickling on my nose woke me up a few hours later. I opened my eyes and grimaced. The sun was up. I must have overslept.

I tried to roll over but I couldn't. I stared at the open window, confused. I turned my head and could see Basil happily eating his breakfast through the open bedroom door.

I heard footsteps and then *he* walked in and sat down.

Slade Kinney was sitting beside me on the bed, fully dressed.

Sipping a cup of coffee.

Meanwhile, I was still naked. And tied up. I tugged on my hands, realizing this wasn't a prank.

*He'd freaking tied me to the damn bed!*

"What- what are you doing?"

He smiled at me patiently.

"Waiting for you to wake up."

"I thought you'd be gone by now."

He narrowed his eyes. He looked…
annoyed with me. *Really annoyed.*

"You did? That's interesting. Well, you were wrong."

"Slade- this really isn't my thing. Can you untie me now please?"

He shook his head slowly.

"No, I don't think I can. Not until we have a little talk."

"About what?"

"I don't want just one night. I want you."

"Slade- this is crazy!"

"Is it?"

He started inspecting his fingernails.

"Yes!"

"Are you saying you didn't enjoy last night?"

I had the grace to blush.

"No but-"

"So you did enjoy it?"

"Yes, of course but-"

"I like you Jenny. A lot. I know you like me."

"I do but-"

He leaned forward and stuffed something in my mouth. My panties. Oh god, it was a pair of my panties. They were clean thankfully, not that it made this any less humiliating

"No 'buts' doll face. It's my turn to talk. And convince you that my way of thinking is best."

He smiled at me and rolled his sleeves up.

"I'm sure we can come to some sort of agreement."

# CHAPTER 14

## SLADE

I*'m not going to make this easy on her. Why should I?*

I stared down at the buxom beauty spread out on the bed. She wasn't going to kick me to the curb, dammit. I wasn't a one night stand.

I was boyfriend material dammit.

More- I was husband material!

I might seem calm on the outside but inside I was burning with indignation. I'd never been rejected in my entire life and it made me angry. Even worse, I was afraid.

I'd never been afraid to lose anyone before.

But I was afraid to lose her. Terrified really. I'd just found Miss Jenny Cakes. She made me feel alive in all sorts of unexpected ways.

Not to mention the *very* expected ways.

I couldn't lose that. I couldn't lose *her*.

So I'd just have to convince her.

I smiled. It wasn't a friendly smile. It was the smile of a predator. A lion who had just spied a particularly juicy gazelle.

With precise movements I rolled up the sleeves of my button-down shirt.

And then I got to work.

I slowly pulled the sheet down off of her very nude, very spread eagle body.

Jesus, but she looked good. Her body was poetry in motion. I'd thought that the first time I saw her, and it still rang true. Curves on curves.

I pulled up something I'd kept hidden just out of sight on the floor. It was an oil. I smirked as I looked at the label. Organic coconut oil.

So Jenny was health conscious. That was adorable.

It was also perfect for my purposes.

I'd found it in the cupboard and had all kinds of ideas... She must use it for baking. I shook my head. Little did she know, it had many, *many* other uses.

I slowly unscrewed the cap and scooped out a handful with my fingers. Then I knelt at her feet and started to rub it in.

"Hmmmffff!"

She wiggled this way and that, clearly ticklish. I was methodical though. Using both hands to hold her still as I rubbed every inch of her.

She moaned in ecstasy as I worked her arches. Then she grumbled angrily at me again. Then another moan.

I ignored her, slowly massaging my way up her legs to her thighs. For a long time I worked on her thighs, coming close to, but not touching her plump little pussy lips.

Well, maybe a little. Just a light skim with the back of my hand, my fingertips. Enough to make her jump off the bed. Enough to make her tight little slit start to drip.

I licked my lips while staring at her petals.

I knew she was watching me like a hawk.

I leaned forward and blew on her.

Her hips jerked and she let out a little moan.

I started rubbing her hips and belly, bypassing her pussy altogether. I was going to play with her until she was out of her mind. She knew it too.

Oh yes, Jenny had just figured out my plan.

I smirked at the furious look in her eyes. Soon, she'd look different altogether.

*She'd look desperate.*

I worked my way up and over her rib cage, brushing her nipples once, twice, three times. I moved upward stroking her neck, shoulders and scalp.

And then I started back down again.

Now she was whimpering softy, her body arching under my tender ministrations. This time I caressed her breasts, fondling them and tweaking the nipples, but only for a minute. When I got to the secret place between her legs, I leaned forward and slid my tongue against her.

Just once.

Then I started on her legs again. Finally I knelt at her feet, lightly running my hands up and down the soles. She was writhing on the bed. I knew I should take pity on her, let her speak.

I could at least give her a chance to beg.

But not yet.

I was too pissed off that she'd wanted to dump me. I couldn't help it. I wanted to make her suffer a little.

And more than that, I wanted to prove a point.

Again, I started massaging my way up her legs. This time when I got to her sopping wet pussy I spent a bit more time licking her. She was whimpering by the time I stopped, lifting my eyes to hers.

I smiled and lowered my head, sucking her clitoris into my mouth. She screamed as I danced my tongue against it rapidly. When I stopped after a few minutes the sound she made was one of pure animal desire.

I smiled as I worked slowly up to her tits again. Now I caressed them fully, suckling one nipple and then the other. She was making urgent sounds, muffled by the panties I'd stuffed in her mouth.

I knew what she wanted and I was not going to give it to her. Instead I spent ten minutes playing with her luscious breasts, driving her to the brink and past it again.

Finally I looked up at her.

She looked flushed and utterly wild.

Perfect.

I smiled.

"Had enough?"

Jenny nodded vigorously.

"Hmmmmfffff!"

I grabbed the edge of her panties and slowly pulled them from her mouth. She panted, staring at me with passion glazed eyes.

"You bastard."

"Uh uh uh. That's no way to get what you are after…"

I held the panties, acting as if I was going to stuff them back into her mouth.

"Please…"

"What do you want? This?"

I dragged my finger down her body to her quivering sex, circling my finger on her clitoris.

"Unnfff… yes…"

"Does that mean you want me?"

"Yes…"

"Say it Jenny. You want me."

"I want you. Please, Slade!"

I pulled my hand away, making her whimper.

"But this was just a one time thing. That's what you said isn't it?"

"Yes- I mean - no! Oh God…"

I traced a lazy circle around her pussy, not quite touching her most sensitive parts. I could see her sex quaking, desperate for my touch.

"So you changed your mind? You are going to see me again?"

"Yes! Whatever you want… Just please… Ohhhh…"

I circled my thumb on her bud again, making her cry out.

"Whatever I want? *Whenever* I want?"

She nodded breathlessly.

"Yes… Yes, Slade…"

"I'm not sure I believe you."

"I mean it! I promise."

I licked my finger and slid it inside her, plumbing her depths. She was so tight but oh so slippery. I wouldn't have a hard time getting inside her this time.

"Swear on Basil."

"Oh FUCK! Yes! I swear. I swear on Basil!"

I laughed and pulled back again.

"Alright then Jenny. I'll give you what you want. What we both want."

She watched me as I pulled my clothes off. I wasn't in a hurry. I was as turned on as she was but I had far more control, more experience.

And I was going to use it.

When my cock sprang free her mouth opened. I smiled and climbed on top of her, guiding my cock to her soaking wet pussy.

"You are sure this is what you want, Jenny?"

She nodded.

"Yes."

I pushed forward, sliding all the way in one long slow thrust.

"I'm not after a fling Jenny. You can't just use me and get away with it."

I pulled back and drove home again.

"Uh-uh- alright. Oh God… I'm sorry."

"That's better."

I circled my hips again, starting to create a tempo. Beneath me I could feel her starting to come. I chuckled. That was fast.

Her head thrashed on the pillow as I continued my leisurely pace. I'd let her come, but not as hard as she would have if I fucked her hard and fast. Plus, this way it would drag on a hell of a lot longer.

And I'd get the answers I wanted.

"I really like fucking you, Jenny. Do you like it too?"

"Oh GOD! YES!"

"Hmmm... that's good. Because I'm going to be doing a lot of it. You'd like that wouldn't you, Jenny?"

I pistoned a little faster now, as her orgasm continued to tear through her. She was mindless but I still insisted she answer me.

I pulled almost completely out, holding my cock right at her entrance. She was still trying to finish, still quivering. Her eyes snapped open and her hips rose. But I pulled back again.

"Jenny?"

"Yes! Yes, I would like that- oh GOD!"

She screamed as I slipped my cock back inside her.

"That's a good girl... hmmmm very good..."

I started my measured thrusts again. I pumped my cock slowly in and out of her for another half hour or so, bringing her to at least five more orgasms. She was practically weeping when I felt my balls tighten up with my load.

During that half hour I'd made her agree to a lot of things.

A lot of delightfully filthy things.

Starting with moving in with me next door.

Basil too of course.

I groaned as my cock jerked inside her, spewing my load deep against her womb.

This time I didn't even bother to pull out.

After all, that was one of the promises she'd made.

She'd promised to give me a baby, too.

Later, when I had untied her and was holding her tenderly in my arms, I whispered in her ear.

"You really made me work for it."

She smiled against my shoulder and shrugged.

"You're worth fighting for, Jenny Cakes."

"Thanks."

I smacked her ass. Then I grabbed it and squeezed. She didn't seem to mind. I'd worn her out to the point that all her hard edges were softened. That was the secret to managing this difficult but magnificent woman.

My woman.

I smacked her bottom again.

It was a very, very nice ass.

And now, it was mine.

"That smells incredible."

I leaned over Jenny's shoulder, peering at her work. Some sort of cookies, though healthy ones of course. I let my hand wander to her front and circled her delicious belly.

My Jenny Cakes was pregnant. We'd been busy this past Summer and Fall. I'd written my next album and was in the process of recording it in the basement studio,

But Jenny had been even busier. Not just keeping me pleased, though I was still insatiable for her. In fact, she'd started a whole new business.

Jenny Cakes Lite.

Healthy snacks for expectant moms and even kids. Healthy, organic and with added nutrients like protein from peas and all kinds of crazy stuff. The local market was carrying it, and she'd even been talking to some major distributors about expanding.

It was exciting stuff, but nowhere as exciting as what we had cooked up together.

Our baby.

And I had another little surprise up my sleeve for my girl.

I kissed my way down her back, over her cute little dress and the stretchy leggings she wore underneath. I paused to take a nip of her heiny and smiled as she spun around.

To find me on my knees in the middle of the kitchen.

I smiled at the shocked expression on her beautiful face. Her eyes were confused. Until I pulled out the box.

And opened it.

Then she slapped her hand over her mouth, leaving a bit of organic oat flour behind. I smiled tenderly as I opened the box. Her eyes were wide as she stared at the rock inside it.

I'd gone all out, with one big-ass diamond.

"Slade…"

"Will you marry me, Jenny?"

Her voice was barely a whisper as she said yes. She nodded as tears ran over her cheeks. It cleaned up most of the flour but not all of it.

I was grinning as I swept her into my arms, kissing her soft lips, flour and all.

"I can't believe it."

"Can't believe what?"

My Jenny was still crying, still soft and sweet in my arms as I wiped off her lovely face.

"I can't believe I'm going to be Mr. Cakes."

## STOP!

Please do NOT go back to the beginning of this book before closing it. If you do, the book will not count as being read and the author will not be credited.

Please use the TOC (located in the upper left hand of your screen) to navigate this book. If you're zoomed out, please tap the center of the screen to ensure you are out of page flip mode.

This is true for all authors enrolled in Kindle Unlimited and as such, this message will appear in all of our books that are enrolled in Kindle Unlimited.

Thank you so much for understanding,
Pincushion Press

# ACKNOWLEDGMENTS

Credits:
    LJ Anderson, Mayhem Cover Design
    Just One More Page Book Promotions
    Pincushion Press

# ABOUT THE AUTHOR

Thank you for reading *Ride With The Devil*! If you enjoyed this book please let me know on by reviewing and on and <u>Goodreads</u>! You can find me on <u>Facebook</u>, <u>Twitter</u>, or you can email me at: <u>JoannaBlakeRomance@gmail.com</u>

Sign up for my <u>newsletter</u>!

Other works by Joanna Blake:

*BRO'*

*A Bad Boy For Summer*

*PLAYER*

*PUSH*

*GRIND* (Man Candy Trilogy Book One)

*HEAT* (Man Candy Trilogy Book Two)

*DEEP* (Man Candy Trilogy Book Three with extended epilogues)

*Go Long*

*Go Big*

*Cockpit*

*Hot Shot*

*Stud Farm* (The Complete Delancey Brothers Collection)

*Torpedo*

*Cuffed*

*Wanted By The Devil (Devil's Riders)*
*Hunter (Joanna Blake Singles)*

COMING SOON:

The Continuation of Mason and Cain's stories
The last book in the Devil's Riders Trilogy

Turn the page for excerpts from Joanna Blake's *Cuffed, Cockpit, Go Long, GRIND, BRO' and A Bad Boy For Summer.*

# CUFFED

I went inside and took a look around. The bar was nearly empty. They must have been closing up when the bike went up in flames. Everyone had taken off after that.

Everyone but the staff.

I saw Mason with his hand resting possessively on a girl's shoulder. She sat at the bar, her arms wrapped around her protectively. I could only see her profile but even that was enough to stop me in my tracks.

All thoughts of murder flew from my head.

The girl was beautiful.

Not just a little bit pretty, or cute, or even sexy. She was fucking gorgeous. With long, wavy, light brown hair, and a delicate profile with a nose that was just the slightest bit turned upwards. Her figure looked slim and athletic, but with curves in all the right places.

She turned to look at me and my breath stopped. My heart seemed to pause, waiting for my mind to catch up with my eyeballs, which felt like they were bugging out of my damn head.

*She was a Goddamned angel.*

Even in this smokey juke joint, with the dim lights and neon beer signs, I could see her eyes.

They were the brightest, deepest blue I'd seen in my life. And I was a fan of staring at the sky, or I had been when I had less shit to worry about.

This was the blue of *ten thousands* skies.

She blinked and I came back to myself. The girl might have the face of an angel but right now she was part of a crime scene. If she worked here, she most likely knew the killer, or at least served him a bucket of wings.

Which meant under my rules, she was part of the problem. The fact that I had such a strong reaction to her only pissed me off. Why the hell work here with all the criminals when she could be plastered all over billboards and magazine covers?

Because she was one of them. The enemy. The ones who had killed Danny.

*Remember that, Conn.*

I forced myself to ignore the hot pulse of lust that was throbbing in my belly and crossed the bar. I flashed my badge and pulled out a tiny note pad. Yeah, I was old school in that way too.

"Name."

"They already interviewed me."

"Not you."

They exchanged a glance and Mason stepped in front of her.

"She ain't got nothin' to do with this, DeWitt."

I let myself steal another look at her. Her huge eyes were looking down at the ground. Her juicy bottom lip was caught between Chiclet white teeth. I squinted at Mason and asked again.

"Name."

"It's okay, Mase."

She cleared her throat and Mason sighed heavily, stepping aside. I was once again struck by the girl's absolute physical perfection. And the nervous look in her eyes.

*Good.*

She should be fucking nervous. I wasn't going to go easy on her because she was stunningly beautiful. Or young. Or scared.

I realized belatedly that the girl looked more than scared. She was frightened out of her mind. That made me want to tell her that everything would be okay. That I would take care of everything for her.

I frowned, disquieted by the swirl of protective and animalistic urges that she was causing. Unwanted urges, dammit.

"Casey. Casey Jones."

Her voice was soft and sweet, stirring something even warmer inside me. But something felt off. It felt like a lie. Maybe it wasn't her real name. I leaned against the bar, musing over how young she looked.

*Too young for me.*

The thought caught me off guard. Now where the hell had that come from? Completely out of left field. Not only was it true, but I certainly didn't date criminal trash.

I glanced at Mason who was frowning at me, a worried look on his face. He cared about the girl, that much was obvious. I had a moment of pure animal jealousy, wondering if he was screwing her.

Why I cared, I had no fucking idea.

But I did. I cared a lot.

I gave Mason a hard look.

"Is she your wife?"

"No."

"Girlfriend?"

He shook his head and some of the tension left my body. I felt a strange relief that made no sense at all. I should not give a damn one way or the other.

But I was almost friendly as I nodded to Mason.

"Then you have to step away, Mason. Sorry."

"I'm responsible for her, dammit!"

Well, that was unexpected. Maybe she was his kid. I looked at her again. Hmm, no. He wasn't *that* much older.

Unless he had a kid at fourteen.

"Is she your child? Relation?"

He shook his head. I glanced at the girl, my eyes skimming over her graceful curves. She really was perfect. She looked like one of those girls in those sexy bra commercials.

Lush and young and desirable.

And way too clean and innocent to be in a place like this. But she wasn't innocent. At the very least, she was a prime witness.

"Is she underage?"

"I'm old enough to work here. I don't serve drinks."

I felt something hitch in my stomach at that. Damn, she *was* young. Not even twenty-one.

I definitely shouldn't be having the sort of thoughts I was having. Thoughts about touching her. Kissing her. Taking her to my bed and tangling up the sheets.

No. I should not be thinking any of that, dammit. And not just because she was involved in a crime.

Not just because she was so young either.

She was one of *them*. The people who had killed my partner.

I'd just met the girl. Never before in my life had I taken one look at a female and thought- I would like to hold her all night.

Not just all night either. I had a crazy feeling I'd like to hold her a lot longer than that.

*Well, fuck.*

# COCKPIT

I licked the sauce off my fingers, watching Jenny work. Feldon had been right. This place *did* have the best barbeque south of the Mississippi.

But the amazing ribs were not half as good as the view.

Sweet Jesus, Jenny was finer than what I'd conjured up in my imagination. Her legs were just as long as I remembered but the rest of her was... different. She'd filled out even more, keeping that hourglass shape that drove me nuts last time we'd met. And then some.

She was a brick house.

And I would love to have a visit inside. Hell, not a visit. I wanted to take up permanent residence.

Too bad she wasn't as happy to see me as I was to see her.

I frowned, rubbing my face. I had to wonder why that was. Maybe she'd asked around about me... Yeah, that would do it.

I had quite a reputation amongst the Marines.

But I was a reformed man now. Or I would be, if she gave me another shot. I tilted my head, wondering why she was here. Again. Off another base.

My eyes got wide. I must be an idiot. She was either a military groupie or had a family member in the service. Just... which one? Husband? No. She wasn't wearing a ring and she didn't strike me as the cheating type. Parent? She wasn't *that* young.

It wasn't falling into place for me. Sweet little Jenny was a mystery. I would figure it out though. And I would make her mine. Or at least soften her up enough to take another crack at it.

If she was a groupie, I didn't care. There were women who had a thing for soldiers, officers in particular. I'd convert her to a one man woman. Just like she'd done to me, the first time I saw those emerald eyes of hers. Hell, if she let me, I'd stick to her like glue.

If she was... related to someone... or an Army brat... well, I might be in bigger trouble than I realized.

I might have to contend with a big brother or a daddy, whoever the unlucky bastard was. I tried to imagine having a daughter that looked like Jenny. It would be hell. Especially since she did not seem to know her effect on men.

And she was innocent enough to work in a place like this and think she wouldn't be dealing with a hard dick or twelve every damn minute. I started getting upset just thinking about it. This was no place for a sweet girl like her. It wasn't safe.

I was going to have to protect her. I'd see her home each night, starting tonight. Hopefully, back to my place.

To my bed.

And that's all there was to it.

I watched as she 'accidentally' spilled a glass of water on a customer. I grinned. He must've said something cheeky to her. So, maybe she could take care of herself.

Didn't mean she didn't need backup.

And I was just the man for the job.

She went behind the bar and picked up a huge box of empties. I was across the room in a flash. I was grinning as I tried to take the box from her.

"I got this sweetheart."

"Let go!"

"What? Why? No need to trouble your pretty little arms."

"My *what?*"

Oh boy. Her eyes were green fire as she wrenched the box out of my hands and flounced into the back. I followed her, a little less confident than I'd been a few minutes ago.

"What's wrong, sweetheart? What got you so riled up?"

She spun around and hissed at me. Like a pissed off kitty cat. I leaned against the door and grinned. I liked kitties. Especially gorgeous ones like her.

"I need this job, Jagger! Don't ruin it for me like you-"

I straightened up. This was not regular grade anger. This was a bonafide grudge.

"Like I what?"

She scowled at me mutinously.

"Nothing."

I smiled again.

"Well, if it reall is nothing, when are you going to let me take you out again?"

"How about never?"

"Oh come on sweetheart, we had a good time together, didn't we?"

She looked like she was about to cough. Or choke. Her eyes were wide, practically bulging, as she seemed to struggle for air. I was about to get her a glass of water when she burst out laughing.

And kept laughing.

She laughed so hard she had to bend forward and rest her hands on her knees.

I stopped smiling.

"What's so damn funny?"

"You are Jagger. I'm surprised you even remember me with all your floozies."

"I don't have any floozies."

I glanced at the heavens, expecting lightning to strike.

"Well, not anymore."

She just looked at me. I could see I'd hurt her somehow. I didn't like that.

Not one bit.

"Come on sweetheart, let's talk."

"I can't. And don't call me that."

I raised an eyebrow at her.

"You can't talk? You're doing just fine."

"No, I mean not here. I'm not supposed to... fraternize."

"Says who?"

She sighed.

"My boss, that's who."

# GO LONG

"How do you like our campus so far Kyle?"

Kyle smiled benignly at my mother. He looked as innocent as a choirboy. Meanwhile, under the table his foot was brushing mine. I wasn't sure if it was deliberate until he did it again. I scowled at him as he oozed charm and good will. All false of course.

I wasn't fooled.

"It's the most beautiful I've ever seen. And the students have been... very friendly."

He grinned at me pointedly and popped a bite of food into his mouth. He made it clear he was talking about me as his foot caressed mine again. I kicked him and he nearly choked. I smiled serenely as my father pounded his back.

Kyle glared at me as he wiped his mouth.

I gave him a look that clearly said 'two can play at that game.'

"Thank you Coach."

"Make sure you chew your food, boy. Can't lose you before the season starts!"

I put my chin on my hand and smiled sweetly. I knew more about sports than most men. But Kyle didn't know that. I intended to milk it.

"Daddy, isn't it unusual to put a walk-on on the team?"

"Hardly ever happens at this level. But Kyle here is an unusual young man."

"He is?"

"He's unnaturally talented on the field Bellie. His military training had a lot to do with it, but some people are just naturals."

"Bellie?"

Kyle's eyes were glowing mischievously. I could have screamed. My plan to control the conversation had completely backfired. If he started calling me 'Bellie' I would lose it. I really would.

"That's what we call our little girl. Did you know they actually pay her to attend school? She had a full ride of course, but they actually give her a stipend and all sorts of administrative jobs for extra money. She has career academic written all over her."

I groaned inwardly. Did he have to make me sound like a cross between a 12 year-old and a grandma? That's what I was really.

Kyle was right when he called me Miss Priss. Just a little girl who acted like the biggest, most responsible, boring goodie two-shoes ever to walk the face of the-

Kyle was staring at my breasts. Not just staring either. He licked his lips and made an appreciative grimace. Like he couldn't stand being this close to me and not touching me.

I coughed, nearly spitting out my mashed potatoes.

He was touching me with his eyes. It was practically foreplay! I tried to ignore him but it was too late. A hot pool of lust had settled in my belly. I crossed my arms, realizing my nipples were hard. I jumped up, knocking over my glass of iced tea.

Thankfully it was almost empty.

"Bellie! Are you alright?"

"Just- chilly. I want to grab a sweater."

"Alright but come right back and we can clear the table."

"Yes, mom."

I practically ran from the room. I could feel Kyle's eyes boring into my back. I heard him ask where the restroom was and excuse himself.

Argh!!! He was following me!

I ran for my bedroom and started to slam the door but he caught it with the flat of his hand.

"Where are you running to... Bellie?"

He was grinning at me like the cat that ate the canary. I had the sudden urge to smack the smug look off his handsome face. His eyes slid over my body, even more blatantly than before. I grabbed a light cardigan, angrily pulling it over my arms. I buttoned the center of it.

"Don't call me that!"

He just shook his head, leaning against my doorframe.

"Why not? You know I can still see those perfect tits of your, Bellie. Your nipples are practically poking a hole through that sweater."

I gasped.

"My father will hear you!"

He grinned.

"No. He won't."

He stepped into my room and I stepped backwards until my back was against the wall. He loomed over me, saying nothing.

Then he ran his hands over my shoulders, deliberately brushing my breasts with his forearms.

"Did I do that to you, Miss Priss?"

I opened my mouth but no words came out. He was making me confused dammit! And he *had* done this to me... without even touching me, I was aroused like never before.

Well, like only *once* before anyway.

"Meet me tomorrow after practice at my dorm. Unless you want me to tell him what you've been up to."

I glared at him.

"Blackmail? Really?"

He nodded slowly.

"I will stoop to anything to get what I want, Bellie. What we both want."

I inhaled sharply as he leaned forward, his lips brushing my ear. I closed my eyes, feeling my heart thud in my chest. My whole body felt alive. I could feel the heat rolling off him. The strength. I could smell that clean manly scent... images of our night together flooded my mind against my will. I whimpered, ready to fall into his arms. All he had to do was kiss me.

But he didn't. He just breathed four soft words against my ear, sending shivers down my spine. At that moment, even my goosebumps had goosebumps.

*"And I want you."*

When I opened my eyes, he was gone.

# GRIND

Something wet slid against my ear. I brushed it away, still half asleep. It grazed my skin again and I rolled away from it. I tried to wipe it off on the pillow beneath my head, grimacing at the slimy sensation. Now I was awake and I didn't want to be.

<u>Damn.</u>

I opened my eyes to see a woman bending over me. Her long blond hair brushed my face. I turned my head away.

"Cut it out."

She sat up, glaring at me.

"You didn't seem to mind last night."

Normally, I would have soothed her. Called her by name. Trouble is, I had no fucking clue who the hell she was.

I looked around.

I had no idea <u>where</u> I was either.

"Fuck me."

She grinned at me, tossing that long bleached hair over her shoulder.

"I already did."

Belatedly I noticed that she was wearing some serious lingerie. Black and cream lace. It matched her bedroom. Her very expensive looking bedroom.

I was swimming in a sea of neutral toned sheets and blankets. Silk probably. Expensive, definitely.

"I'd like to again."

I shook my head.

"Sorry babe, I gotta go."

She pouted. I rolled out of bed, looking for my clothes.

"Oh come on... Didn't we have fun together last night?"

I smiled and nodded. It's not that she was bad looking, even if she was at least a decade older than me. It was hard to tell with these rich older broads. She was toned, buffed and polished to a high shine.

Well preserved didn't even begin to cover it.

Yeah, she was hot. Not just for a cougar. But I wasn't in the mood. I didn't usually go for seconds anyway.

Hell. I never did.

Hit it and quit it was my motto. It served me well. I didn't want any entanglements and I doubted I ever would.

I looked at her, giving my best impersonation of someone who gave a shit.

"Where are my clothes?"

She smiled back and shrugged.

"I really couldn't say."

<u>Fucking hell.</u>

"That's great. Just great."

I looked around the room, lifting cushions and opening drawers. Nada. On the bedside table were my keys, wallet and phone. I scooped them up, thanking God for small favors.

"Have a nice day, Ma'am."

"Wait- you aren't leaving like that!"

I coyly waved bye bye to her and left. I jogged through her palatial house in the buff. The marble floors were cool under my feet. The place screamed mega bucks. But not in a tacky way. It was tastefully done, just like the lady herself.

She was chasing me through the house, becoming less composed by the second.

"Seriously, you can't! What will the neighbors think?"

I stopped at the front door of her mansion, glancing back over my shoulder.

"You should have thought of that before you hid my shit."

She screamed in frustration and threw a vase at me. I heard it shatter against the door as I closed it behind me. Just in the nick of time.

"Damn. That would have left a mark."

I made a call as I strolled down her manicured driveway to the gate.

"Joss, can you pick me up? I need a ride."

I leaned against the wrought iron gate and waved at a neighbor who was walking their dog.

"Take your time."

# BRO'

Not one for slacking I started my first full day home with a match against the club pro Matt. It cost extra to play with him but I didn't care. He was an amazing player and gave as good as he got. And for some reason, he considered me a friend.

Probably because most of the people who hired him were bored housewives hoping to get into his pants.

I'd noticed the cougar crowd dropping me hints the past few years as well. And now that I was 21... well maybe I'd take one of them up on it. At least I could be sure an older woman would know what she was doing.

I was dripping with sweat by the time we were done. I wasn't a big fan of showering at the club so I left. Matt waved me off and begged me to book him as much as possible this summer. I promised I would.

What the fuck else was I supposed to do?

Except, well, <u>fuck.</u>

As much as possible.

As many girls as possible.

Speaking of which maybe I'd text Jen later. I knew she was waiting on me. I did enjoy working out horizontally, especially with a sexy female like Jen. She liked to sport fuck as much as I did.

I was turning down our driveway in my convertible when I hit the breaks.

Hard.

A girl was biking toward me. From the general direction of the house. Long dark blond hair blew behind. Big high tits filled out her t-shirt admirably. She had a teeny tiny waist and long tanned legs. She rode closer and I tried to get a look at her face.

Pretty, that much was obvious, with big beautiful eyes. I could see her puffy lips from twenty feet away. Cute little nose too.

The girl looked like a God damned swimsuit model.

<u>No. Wait. What.</u>

My brain went utterly blank as I realized something.

It was Mouse. Mouse was the swim suit model. I was staring at Mouse with lust.

Hot, unrelenting lust.

I jolted to action as she pulled up by my car.

"Nev?"

She stopped her bike, those impossibly long legs straddling the seat. Her jean shorts were short, almost up to the top of her perfect thighs. I swallowed, realizing my mouth was a little bit dry.

But my dick was throbbing.

She smiled at me, cool as a cucumber. Where was the worshipful little Mouse I knew and loved?

"Hey Clay."

She'd grown up obviously. And she'd grown up right.

Still, I knew how to charm the pants off a girl, no matter how hot she was. And I wanted to. I knew it instantly. I wanted to fuck Mouse, of all people.

Really, really bad.

I smiled, letting my eyes wander over that ridiculously perfect little body.

"Where you going?"

She tossed her head, sending a cascade of wavy blond hair over her shoulder. It was very sexy, but not deliberate or coy. She was unconsciously seductive. It was hypnotizing.

"Job hunting."

I smirked.

"In that outfit?"

She looked down at herself and back at me.

I pulled my sunglasses down and switched gears.

"I think you've outgrown those shorts little Mouse."

Then I drove away. Slowly. Very slowly.

Just so I could check out her ass in the rear view window.

Good lord, the girl was fine. She'd stop traffic anywhere. No matter what she was wearing.

I went into the house to change, all thoughts of texting Jen forgotten.

# A BAD BOY FOR SUMMER

I threw my arm over the back of the seat and looked to the side, letting my eyes slide over her body. Frannie didn't seem to notice. Her hands were gripping the bar that had locked us into place in the Ferris wheel seat.

I leaned back and watched her as the ride started to spin.

She looked like a little kid, nervous and excited. Her cheeks were pink and her eyes sparkled when she turned to look at me.

"I thought you didn't like Ferris wheels."

"I don't! I'm petrified."

I grinned at her.

"I'll protect you."

She laughed as if that were the wittiest thing I could have said. I laughed too, her laughter was that infectious. As soon as we got to the top of the wheel I slid over to her. Her face was startled as she looked into my eyes. My eyes lowered to her soft inviting lips.

I leaned in and tilted my head, angling my mouth against hers.

Her lips felt like pillows underneath mine. Warm and sweet. Her breath mingled with mine as I slowly eased into the kiss, nibbling and licking her until she opened her mouth.

Then the kiss went wild.

My hands reached for her hips as I pulled her against me. Her breasts mashed against my chest and I moaned, diving back into her mouth to tangle my tongue with hers.

I felt like my dick was a fucking rocket, it was so ready to lift off.

The next thing I knew the ride had stopped and a crowd of people were staring at us. I guess we didn't notice. I wanted the ride to go on and on. As it was I had to hold my jacket in front of me as I climbed out.

I glanced at Frannie. Her pretty lips were swollen and pouting. I wanted to get horizontal with her right fucking now.

Jesus Christ, what was she doing to me?

The girl had the moves that was for fucking sure.

I took her hand and pulled her toward the boardwalk, desperately looking for a place to be alone with her. She smiled at me shyly. There was an innocence in her gaze that made me absolutely sure that she had no fucking clue what I had in mind.

I had a sinking feeling that Frannie was a good girl. That her innocence might be a problem. That it might take more than a Ferris wheel ride to get into her pants. It wasn't going to stop me from trying though.

I knew something else too.

I knew it without a doubt.

This girl was going to be mine.

# STOP!

We hope you enjoyed this book and your free excerpts. Please do NOT go back to the beginning of this book before closing it. If you do, the book will not count as being read and the author will not be credited.

Please use the TOC (located in the upper left hand of your screen) to navigate this book. If you're zoomed out, please tap the center of the screen to ensure you are out of page flip mode.

This is true for all authors enrolled in Kindle Unlimited and as such, this message will appear in all of our books that are enrolled in Kindle Unlimited.

Thank you so much for understanding,
Pincushion Press

74063859R00193

Made in the USA
Columbia, SC
24 July 2017